PIRATE QUEEN'S REVENGE

PIRATE MOST WANTED
BOOK 2

ISOLDE HOLYOAKE

BONNETPUNK PRESS

Pirate Queen's Revenge, by Isolde Holyoake

Published by Anna Klein, Bonnetpunk Press

Cover by Lara Wynter

ISBN:

[978-1-0670200-5-7] Paperback

[978-1-0670200-6-4] Erub

[978-1-0670200-7-1] Print on Demand

ACKNOWLEDGMENTS

This book took approximately five years longer to write than I initially planned, because after releasing the first one, I developed debilitating chronic migraines. I want to thank all the readers who enjoyed Pirate Queen's Curse so much that they kept asking for this book, and kept my enthusiasm for the story alive. Not the least of these is my mum, who regularly demanded "more pirate books!"

I want to thank my patient and dedicated editor, Gillian St Kevern, who turned my messy draft into something legible. I couldn't have done this without her keen insight and her support.

I'm so grateful to my Mum, Dad, my sister Judit, and my husband Tigger for all of their constant support in the last few really difficult years in general, and for their specific support with my writing.

Thanks to my friends who keep me sane and encourage me: Michelle, my business buddy, and one of Magpie's biggest fans. And Sarah, Philippa, Prema, Porl, Elle and Tanja. You all rock

To Magpie's three biggest real-world fans:
My mum, Tigger and Michelle

AUTHOR'S NOTE

Firstly, a note on generative AI: **This book is entirely human made** and no generative AI was used in any part of the process. I believe the arts are for human expression, even if it is something as whimsical as sexy pirate adventures. My editor is a human being. My cover artist is human being who does not use AI elements in her work. I realise there is an abundance of em dashes in the text, and I'm afraid that's because I love em dashes and I've loved them long before we were blighted by generative AI. I hope you'll understand that it's just the writing foible of a millennial and not the telltale sign of a soulless plagiarism machine.

Secondly, a note on historical accuracy. Because the 'golden age of piracy' that is depicted here is based on the largely made up fantasy version of piracy we see in movies and books, it's hard to pinpoint a date for historical details. I've used historical detail where I can and for the rest, I've gone with 'vibes'.

1

Hung by the neck until dead.

    Thrown into Shark Bait Bay.

Locked in a room with a poisonous snake

Another day, another island, an all new slew of people to fantasize about murdering.

My vision was still dancing with the after-effects of Magnus Grimstead's light show: an enormous column of purple light and teleportation, the magical equivalent of whipping his dick out and waving it at the biggest gathering of pirates in the Caribbean. Normally, the image of a wizened rich man in magician's robes swinging his old-man dick around would make me laugh but currently, I was so angry, the laughter emerged as a choke of indignation.

They'd kidnapped Val. My best friend. The queen of sex. The jewel of the Caribbean.

"*Fuck!*" I shouted. It came out shriller than I would have liked.

A haze of gunpowder from the naval battle earlier still hung over the town. My night vision was returning. I turned to look at the crowd. Every sailor who could stand unaided after the battle with Haddrick and Mercer's fleet was there. Most of them stood with jaws agape. A few were muttering, mostly to themselves.They all looked at me.

Did they blame me? Or did they just expect me to know what to do next?

I rounded on Lysander. He stood beside me in just his breeches, having been interrupted mid-amorous encounter. His chest was so pale, it was almost as blinding as his dad's magic column.

"You," I growled, grabbing him by the ear, yanking him toward me until we were nose to nose. "Explain what the fuck just happened."

He hissed in pain.

"*Me?*" he said, with a hint of a whine in his voice. "*I* didn't have anything to do with it. Let go of me."

"No." My anger had bubbled over from raging hot to seething cold. I dragged Lysander by the ear toward the epicentre of the magical column, the prison pit at the centre of town. "Why didn't they just fucking take you instead of kidnapping Val?"

"I'm still tied to the ship, for one thing," Lysander said, between noises of irritation and pain. "Secondly, that's not how magic works. It would be *very* bad news if my father could reach across long distances at will and snatch people."

"He literally just did that." I nearly shook him. "You were right there."

We reached the edge of the pit. It looked like an explosion had taken place. The old stones were scorched. Lying in a huddled heap, chained to the floor where I'd last seen her, was my former-first-mate-turned-mutineer, Elspeth. She looked like hell. Her clothes were in tatters and ugly burns

2

were visible across most of her skin. I couldn't tell if she was dead or alive, until she shifted slightly.

Alive then, at least for the moment.

"Do you see the pattern of the burns?" Lysander said, his hand coming up to grip my wrist and try to free his ear. I tightened my hold. "She's the centre, they all streak out from her. She must have had a magical focus. Father's work is usually exceptionally neat, so my wager is that he was using something she had for a purpose different than the one initially intended."

"She had some ugly necklaces." I peered at her. "They're gone now." Other than the burns left in great looping lines where they had lain against her skin.

"Probably the focus," Lysander said. "Almost certainly designed to pull her out rather than bring people through."

"Wish I'd thrown them in the sea." I stared at Elspeth's prone form. "But I didn't think they were important."

"If it makes you feel better," Lysander offered, still trying to free his ear from my pinch, "that probably wouldn't have helped much."

I turned to face the rumbling crowd of pirates, and addressed them with a well practiced boom.

"If these scurvy bilgerats want me to come to Port Elizabeth, then by Neptune's hairy blue nutsack, they're going to get me in Port Elizabeth," I announced to the mass of wounded, drunk, and gobsmacked pirates gathered in the streets, trying very much to sound like I had some fucking idea I knew what I was doing. "And they're going to fucking regret inviting me, they're going to fucking regret blackmailing me and most of all they're going to regret ever thinking they could lay a hand on Val."

The crowd roared, all concentrated anger. My rage

3

swelled in answer. "I have the old wizard's son here by the ear and the commodore locked in my brig. If they want these two assholes back, well, we'll serve them up on a platter with a side order of revenge besides. Drink, fuck, rest. But in the morning, any sailor who wants to take up this invitation to Port Elizabeth, be ready: we sail on the noon tide, and we will show them what it means to steal from the thieves."

2

———

The conclusion of my rallying cry brought a loud roar. The crowd began to disperse. The hum of victory now had an undercurrent of unease and unsettled stirring.

"Your old man kicked a hornet's nest. Do you think he knows that?" I asked Lysander, yanking on his ear.

He hissed with pain. "He kicked an anthill. You might *think* you're hornets, but you're helpless against him."

"We'll see," I muttered. " Let's look at this mess. You're going to tell me exactly what your daddy's pyrotechnics were all about."

I finally released his ear and climbed down into the pit, taking in the detritus of Magnus's magic. Lysander scrambled after me, proving he had some sense after all. A third set of boots landed near us. I looked back to see the tall form of Benedict St Stephen, a commodore of the British Navy and currently my prisoner.

"*A prisoner in your brig?* You didn't need to protect me like that," the commodore said. "I have been more than willing to own up to who I am."

"Yeah?" I hiked an eyebrow. "I'm sure you've already tried telling them who you are. How'd that go?"

There was a long pause.

"They didn't believe me," he admitted. "They like me." The admission pained him.

"Well, don't look at me for an explanation." I shrugged and turned back to look at the blasted pit. "I for one don't like you."

"Sure, that's why you protected him," Lysander said. I could hear the sneer in his voice and my palm itched to slap him.

"I was protecting my own ass."

"Is that why you've been flirting with him non-stop?"

Don't murder the smug little git. Don't murder him. You need him.

"You don't have to like someone to want to fuck them. You nearly managed to get some action and you're completely unlikeable."

"I'm very likeable. You just have no taste."

"You're not likeable, Grimstead," the commodore interjected. "But Flint still has no taste."

"All right, I'm done with listening to what passes for witty repartee from the two of you. I'm in a lot of pain, I'm very angry, I really want to kill someone for this, and Dauntless turned into a parrot right before I finally managed—" I cut myself off. "...you know what, that's not relevant. The two of you are going to help me examine this mess, then go nice and quiet back to the ship, and then I'm going to get some sleep. I have a lot of revenge to deal with in the morning. Am I understood?"

Suddenly, Elspeth moved. She let out a horrendous,

rasping sound, somewhere between a cry and a groan. The three of us jumped.

I grabbed Lysander by the arm, digging my fingers in hard enough to bruise." Is there anything else magical on her person?"

"There's nothing on her person except burns. Even you should be able to tell that."

The commodore stared across the pit, jaw working as he looked at Elspeth. He met my eyes. "She's still alive."

The most law-abiding man I've ever met—though that's not saying much, given my usual company—was far from his usual state of regulation cleanliness. He wore dark breeches and a shirt stained by dirt and blood from the earlier battle. His short shorn dark hair was matched by several days of stubble. That, coupled with the heat of anger behind his blue eyes, made him look more like a bloodthirsty pirate than the representative of the law on the sea.

"Aye," I said. "Fucking Grimstead couldn't do us the courtesy of finishing her off."

"Leave it to me, captain." The commodore surged forward with a singular look of focus.

I knew that look in a man's eyes. It meant murder.

3

My free hand shot out, grabbing him by the wrist. "Hold on now, matey," I snapped.

He rounded on me. "I want her dead." His voice was guttural, raw.

Instead of making me angry, as it should have, it sent a shiver up my spine. Something tightened low in my abdomen. Vengeful made him look intensely fuckable. I wasn't ready for the hot rush of lust, especially not in the midst of disaster.

The commodore wrenched me from my thoughts, trying to shake off my hand. "I thought you wanted her dead too."

Didn't I want her dead? She was a mutineer, former first mate, a long time friend who stabbed me and most of us pirate folk in the back...

Yeah. I should want her dead.

Sympathy pierced my stomach. I knew why he wanted her dead. She killed his crew and sank his ship.

We should be fighting over who got to kill her. I shouldn't be stopping him. So why was I?

"We won't be killing her," I told him. "She has information and she knows where my old crew is. We still need her."

"I don't understand you at all." His confusion was palpable. I could feel him trembling with rage, rage with no outlet. Join the club, sailor.

"You'll thank me later," I said. "For stopping you from murdering a woman without a proper trial. You'd hate yourself after the rage wore off. I'm doing you a favour."

"Excuse me," Lysander interrupted. "Do you really need me here while you gaze at each other, yelling about murdering people, or can I get back to where my lovers and I were rudely interrupted?"

Oh good, I was so glad he reminded me he was there, he was much less complicated to be angry about.

"You're not fucking anyone, Grimstead, not with Val kidnapped, not with any of this happening." I released the commodore's wrist, and pointed at Elspeth. "Give me a straight answer. Anything magical left?"

"If there was, it's burned away now. She should be dead. That's probably the only reason they left her behind."

"Then we're done here." I crouched to address Elspeth. "I'm going to put you out of the way where you're not going to bother me or anyone else, and I can keep my eye on you." I turned to the commodore, who was still standing there, his eyes showing rage and confusion. "Commodore, take Elspeth to the brig. See that she's alive when you leave her there." I waited for him to acknowledge the order before I left him there, reasonably confident he wouldn't kill Elspeth. He bowed his head. Satisfied, I hauled myself out of the pit.

Topside, I found Lysander trying to sneak off into the crowd. Any patience I had left ran out in that moment. I dragged him into a headlock, and clamped my hand over his mouth. As I hauled him towards my ship, an amused ripple spread through the crowd of pirates. Lysander tried to fight my grip, but for all his magical powers, his arms hadn't seen a push-up in a good long while.

I bellowed at the crowd. "Someone fetch me my ship's doctor, and Judith the witch."

I strode towards the ship, Lysander's feet scrabbling for purchase before dragging behind us uselessly. He resorted to trying to bite my palm.

Judith appeared at my side as I was pulling him along the gangplank onto the ship, and she helpfully lifted his feet off the ground. I didn't need the help, but let her do it, after all, it was all the more ignominious for Lysander.

"You're not going to kill him, are you?" Judith peered over the tops of the wizard's bare feet. "I have so much magic to learn from him. Oh, and you need him to rescue your friend."

"No, I'm not going to kill him, I've got just the place for him. But I need your advice to make sure he can't cast any spells or do anything spooky while he's meant to be helpless."

The door to my cabin was open. I hadn't shut it when I had gone to investigate the bone-shaking shouting. We hauled Lysander inside, and I dumped him unceremoniously on the floor.

He didn't say anything, for once, just gazed at me petulantly. He reminded me of nothing so much as a cat pushed off a chair. Val's 'parrot cage' had been housing my ex-lover-turned-parrot for the past few days but in reality, it had been constructed with a human sized occupant in mind. I unhooked the lock that held the side shut, and the entire side of the cage opened.

"If I stick him in there, will he be able to do any hocus pocus?" I asked, looking at Judith, whose eyes were a little too wide. You'd think she hadn't seen a person sized cage before. Then again, most people on the right side of the law haven't. Though Val's cage was made with carnal pursuits in mind, it would do just fine keeping a snippy brat of a wizard man in check.

"I don't know why you're asking her," Lysander said archly. "She didn't even know magic was real this afternoon."

"Yet since then she's used magic to animate a dead snake. And I don't trust your opinion." I prodded him with my foot, and looked back at Judith. "So?"

"He's right, I'm not an expert, but given what we've seen tonight it sure seems like they need their magic circles with the chalk and the blood to do anything major."

"Great." I grabbed Lysander by the arms and hauled him into the belly of the cage.

"He's still connected to the ship though," Judith pointed out. "Even in physical form he could do something to affect the ship."

"Yes, see how far you get in your sailing tomorrow with my ass sitting in this cage."

I gripped the far edge of the cage with one hand, and the outer edge with the other, making my body a barrier between him and freedom. He looked up at me with a sneer and mutinous cobalt eyes that held the heat of anger, and just a touch of uncertainty.

"If you stop this ship from sailing, you're going to regret it."

"Oh, I'm certain," he said, with a smile that can be best described as oily. I'd have bet gold that he got this straight from his father. "However. I think tonight demonstrates that we can work together. We have a common interest. You want me to get home, so you can get your friend back. And I want me to get home so I can get back to a life that doesn't involve living as part of a pirate ship. But don't think I'm not aware of the power I have here. You could certainly do well to give me an enticement for good behaviour."

I stared at him. I wondered if I was dead, and I was in some kind of hell, where my punishment was to negotiate with fuckwits nonstop.

"Entice you how?" I asked finally.

"You interrupted my time with my lovers," he said. "I've spent a year incorporeal, trapped in an astral world. I'm sure you could convince one of Val's fine-"

"Not going to happen," I cut in. He looked up at me with mock innocence. "How do you think that conversation is going to go? Hey who wants to fuck the reason your friend and employer is missing?"

"That sounds like a problem for you to solve."

I tried to not grind my teeth. I tilted my head sideways to look at Judith.

"Say, Judith, you like magic— "

Judith was shaking her head before I finished speaking.

"Sorry captain, I only like women." She spread her hands apologetically. "If he were Lysandra, I'd be all over her, but as things stand..."

"Fine," I said. "We'll see if he's got any sisters when we're in Port Elizabeth. In the meantime," I turned back to Lysander, "I hope you enjoy a good hate-fuck, because that's what's on the menu tomorrow. Just you and me and this cage."

Lysander's eyes widened. "You?" He looked me up and down, then let his face relax back into a smirk. "As long as your species doesn't bite the head off their lover at the end of coitus, that sounds fine."

"*Fine?* I'm some damned hot stuff, and anyway who rips the head off their lover?"

"There's a certain kind of spider," Lysander said.

"I'm a pirate, not a bug. You're safe from having your head ripped off. I'm more likely to use a gun."

"Spiders aren't bugs," Lysander seemed compelled to point out. "A bug, or an insect, is an arthropod and has six legs. Spiders are arachnids, and have eight legs." I squinted at him. Fuck me, first the commodore with his lecture on snakes, now this shit? Was everyone around me a secret wildlife expert?

"Listen, Judith, any spells to shut him up?" I asked.

"I'd just gag him if it were me, captain," Judith said. Lysander shot a venomous look over at her—hah, now who's the spider?— but I was already scooping a discarded shirt from the floor. I had no idea whose it was. Maybe it was Dauntless's. Maybe it was the commodore's. It wasn't mine. I roughly gagged him, making sure he had enough room to breathe, then slammed the side of the cage shut.

Lysander, gagged, shirtless, trapped in a gilded cage. After everything that had happened, this was rather satisfying. I smiled sweetly at him as he looked up at me with heat in his eyes. It must have been anger, it had to be anger, but it sent a frisson up my spine. It felt more like lust.

I must have been more tired than I thought.

"Sleep well, Grimstead," I said, grabbing the large black cloth that I used to cover the cage. "See that *The Queen's Liberty* sails nicely and we'll have a hot time tomorrow night." There was a half articulated protest from him as I threw the cloth over the cage.

"Captain, are you really going to fuck him?" Judith asked

as we stepped out of the cabin. She looked at me with her eyebrows arched.

I rubbed my face tiredly. The sun was creeping over the horizon and I had spent the whole night riding adrenaline. I was done. "Hate-fuck, Judith, there's a difference." I looked around for any sign of the commodore or Elspeth.

"I know men aren't my field, but even so, that man is more than a little... blegh."

"You're just saying that because he's a cowardly worm with a terrible family who has done nothing but get us into trouble."

"I find that a pretty big turn off, don't you?"

"Me too, but I'd rather fall on the sword myself, so to speak, than make someone else do it." Judith was opening her mouth to speak again. "Judith, I like you, but I need you to stop asking me questions. Go get some sleep. I'll come see you before we set off."

"One last question," Judith said, holding up a finger. "What do I need to pack?"

"For what?" I stared at her.

"For the journey." I blinked. "I'm coming with you, obviously."

That was news to me but it could wait until morning, I didn't have the energy for an argument.

"I have no idea, I've never had to pack. Everything I own lives on the ship all the time." Judith opened her mouth again. I'm not sure what the expression on my face looked like but it made Judith put up her hands peaceably.

"I'm sure I can figure it out. Sleep well, captain!"

For a few blissful seconds, there was silence. Almost, anyway. I could hear the sea and the chorus of the dawn birds, and the distant singing and shouting of pirates. It was nice. No one was asking me difficult questions or making demands or generally asking more of me than I was capable of at the moment. I hadn't even had time to consider the multitude of heartache I had: more than anything, I wanted to talk to Val about it all. But of course, I couldn't.

On the other hand, I had Elspeth again.

The thought made me laugh out loud, a harsh sound that hurt my throat as it escaped.

Right. Like I'd be confiding anything in Elspeth again. She'd burned the bridge between us so well not even ashes remained.

It occurred to me that I should make sure that the commodore didn't have a sudden fit of lawlessness, and had actually delivered Elspeth to my brig instead of throwing her in the sea. I needed her until I was sure she had no more useful information for me. Val would say I needed her until I had resolved the complicated emotional issues we had, but Val was always talking about feelings. And anyway, she wasn't here. Because of Elspeth. There was nothing complicated about it, I told myself as I climbed down into the hold of the ship as fast as I could. Nothing at all.

4

I would have probably believed my story if I wasn't hit with a crushing wave of relief when I saw Doc and the commodore standing over Elspeth's form in the cell.

My former first mate was laid out on the makeshift bed that lived in the cell. She was wrapped in what appeared to be clean white sheets, doused in water. Doc was mixing up a sweet smelling mixture.

As I got closer, I saw Elspeth was awake.

"They took Val, did you know they were going to do that?"

"No," Elspeth rasped. She shut her eyes. "Supposed to rescue me."

"Sucks to be let down by the people you thought you could count on, doesn't it?"

Elspeth didn't react except to take a slow breath. "Why not kill me?"

"Not until I know where our—MY—original crew is. Not until I know everything from you, everything that could help us get Val back. So don't even think about trying to end yourself. I'll march into hell and drag you out if I have to."

"No," Elspeth said. At first I couldn't tell what she was disagreeing with but once she'd taken another slow breath, she continued. "Not supposed to hurt anyone but you. I'll help."

"Oh good." I didn't bother to hide the bitterness in my voice. "You were *only* supposed to hurt me. Your best friend."

Doc gave me a dirty look—the bad kind, reserved for patients being excessively reckless or people bothering their patients. Elspeth did nothing but take in a slow breath and let it out again. I couldn't tell if it was a sigh, or if that's just how she breathed now that Grimstead the Elder had fucked her up.

The lack of response was getting to me. I was mad. I was so mad at the sheer unfairness of everything that happened in the last week.

"You make sure you get better fast so that you can fix all the fuckups you caused." I took a step closer. I think I hoped I was menacing but getting a better look at her injuries, I wasn't at all sure I could be any worse than what she was going through already.

"Captain, while your grievances are entirely justified, your bedside manner isn't the most effective." Doc looked up from the syrup they were mixing with a narrow wooden spatula.

"What about." Elspeth spoke before I could, her words rattling on her wheezy voice, "your fuckups. Captain."

"You bitch!" I surged forward.

Doc put their hand out to stall me, but it was Commodore St Stephen who bodily blocked my way.

"Captain, I'm going to need you to leave me with the patient," Doc informed me. "She'll be dosed with a painkiller that will make her all but insensible so your conversation will not be able to continue."

I gritted my teeth and glared at Doc. The commodore was too tall for me to see over so I had to peer around his arm. Very menacing.

"You wanted to save her, captain," Doc replied evenly, before turning their attention back to Elspeth. "Let me do my job." Expertly sliding an arm under Elspeth's head, they lifted her up just enough to tip the syrup down her throat. Elspeth made little noises of pain as she drank.

"Let's go, captain, doctor's orders." Benedict St Stephen put a hand on my arm. "You knew I'd regret it if I killed her right now. I know you'd regret it too. Let's all get some rest."

I wrenched my arm out from his hold, and stomped out of the brig and up onto the deck. I felt like I'd been drinking but it was only the exhaustion. The adrenaline was retreating. There was nothing left in my body but pain, anger and grief.

"The watch has been set, captain." It was Peggy, the leader of the deck minnows, balanced expertly on two wooden legs. Since most of the minnows weren't interested in fighting, they'd been left in charge of the morning after. "Townsfolk from Shark Bait Bay are on their way back to relieve the local townsfolk and to begin cleanup. Scouts are watching from the headlands to scan for approaching vessels."

"Good job." I loved it when my instructions were followed. I squinted at the sliver of dawn setting the sea alight, trying to think of any jobs that needed doing. There was nothing. "Seen my parrot anywhere?"

"He's sleeping up in the Crow's Nest. Scamp's keeping an eye on him."

"Good. He's not to be hurt, I've become quite attached to him."

Behind me, the commodore snorted, but Peggy just nodded vigorously. "Yes captain."

With a nod, I dragged myself to my cabin, heaving a sigh of relief as I walked in—until a hand caught the door and prevented it from closing.

5

_____

"What do you think you're doing here?" I demanded of the hand, or rather, the man attached to the hand.

"I sleep here." The commodore raised an eyebrow. "Remember?"

I did, now that he said it. That whole bizarre bunking arrangement felt like it belonged to another age, not just the previous day.

"That was just to protect you from the pirates," I said, not stopping him as he came into the cabin, securing the door behind him. "You're mates with them all now, you'll be fine." I made a vague shooing gesture.

"Maybe I would. But it's been a long night and it's going to be a long few days, so I would rather get a good few hours sleep while I can than try to master the skill of sleeping with one eye open, if it's all the same to you."

"Fine. Make yourself at home." At this point I was so tired that as long as he wasn't murdering me, he could sleep anywhere in the room he wanted, including curled up in bed with me. But I wasn't going to say that out loud. I stomped towards my bed and pulled off my boots with practiced ease.

For a second I wondered, self-consciously, if my feet smelled.

Of course they do. And I hope it's so terrible he leaves.

The bed was rumpled and there was a scattering of red feathers. I glowered, remembering my interrupted sexy-time with Dauntless, once again making a mental note to feed Magnus Grimstead his own balls—

"Flint, can you hear a word I'm saying?"

I jerked out of my thoughts, swaying next to my bed with a boot in hand. Had I fallen asleep while standing?

"What?" My question came out as a half growl. The other half was 'petulant whine' but I was going to cut me some slack on that.

"I *said*, Doc wanted me to look at your back."

"My back."

"Your back. As in, the injuries you sustained thereupon." I must have still looked as uncomprehending as I felt. "As in, the injury that's spreading quite a blood stain on the back of your shirt thus making your ship's doctor concerned you ripped open the stitches, probably by doing something against their sage advice."

As soon as I remembered the injury, all the pain that the adrenaline had been dampening washed over me like a tidal wave and I staggered a little. I *had* noticed my back was damp but I had assumed it was sweat or sea water.

"Sit and lean forward onto the table." St Stephen indicated a stool he'd dragged over from a corner, an ornamental thing with a fancy puff pillow on top and frou-frou lace dangling off the sides. One of Val's many obscure pieces of splendour that somehow ended up in my cabin. I thought it looked ghastly but it still seemed a shame to get blood on it.

"*Magpie Flint.*" This time I jerked awake to find the commodore right in front of me. "Sit down. I admit it has crossed my mind that this would be easier to do if you're out like a light but it doesn't seem ethical."

"What are you talking about?"

"Your back needs to be stitched properly," St Stephen said, his face as serious as the noose. "Doc's busy with Elspeth, so they asked me to do it since I've been trained as a field medic—"

A giggle of disbelief escaped me. "You're wanting to patch me up?"

"Doc was right," he muttered. "You are a dreadful patient."

"You want to see me executed for piracy but you're going to play good Samaritan along the way?"

A line formed between his brows, a sure sign he was getting to the end of his tether. "First of all, I said a fair trial under the law, not your execution. Second of all, right now it's in both our interests that you stay alive, and third of all, would you bloody well sit down, you obnoxious thief."

"Only because you asked so nicely." I sat heavily on the stool. I lied, it wasn't because he asked nicely. It was because my legs were giving out.

He slammed a small corked bottle on the table. "For the pain."

I drank it in one gulp, gagging at the signature taste of Doc's pain remedy. Now that my back was throbbing, and I'd irritated the man that was going to be jabbing a needle into it, I had a feeling I was going to need it.

"Shirt," he instructed crisply.

"Never thought I'd live to see the day." I peeled the blood-soaked garment off my skin and over my head, leaving only dirty bandages wrapped around my torso. "Never thought you'd be ordering me to undress."

"In a strictly *medical* capacity, Flint." I wished I could see his face. It had been a shit night but seeing him blush would help. Instead I had to make do with sensing his hesitation as his hands hovered around the bandages.

"What is this?" he asked disapprovingly. "Old sailcloth?"

"Probably." I started loosening whatever fabric had been spared for bandages. It was all but rags and rapidly fell to the floor. Fresh air hit the open gashes across my back and tightened the nipples on my now exposed breasts.

I waited for a reaction.

Nothing.

I gingerly twisted round on the stool to find Commodore Benedict St Stephen standing there with his eyes squeezed shut.

"Commodore, they're only out in a *medical* capacity."

"If you could spare a thought for my modesty, captain, I would appreciate arranging yourself in a manner that..." He gesticulated vaguely.

This man was really something else.

"I want you to know that I have met nuns less prudish than you," I told him. Once I was hunched over the table, my girls tucked away as best as they could be in my arms, I gave him the all clear. I could actually feel the tension leave him as, I presume, he opened his eyes and found himself not accosted by my bare bosom.

"How did you meet nuns?" the commodore asked. Behind me, I heard water splashing. "Did they survive?"

"It's a long story." I put my forehead down on my arms

and shut my eyes. I didn't feel like sharing my tragic past as an orphan raised by nuns while two of my enemies were in the room, though the snoring emanating from the cage indicated that Lysander was asleep. "Would you believe it if I said the nuns were worse to me than I was to them?"

"I find that hard to believe."

I didn't get a chance for a witty reply, hissing in pain as he started cleaning my back. The water and his movements sent a wall of pain through me. "Fuck, what are you using back there, acid?"

"I should have known you were one of those patients that can take a cannonball on the field but whines like a child in the medic's hands."

"I *know* that trick," I informed him. "I *use* that trick."

"Is it going to work, or am I going to get to tell people that the most wanted pirate in the Caribbean couldn't handle her stitches getting done?" The commodore was doing his best to keep his voice level but there was a tone of smugness in there.

I growled and resettled myself. "You've got me there, commodore."

He chuckled then, a sound I'd never heard from him before. Low, deeply masculine, playful, and definitely smug. It sent a jolt of warmth straight through me, striking low in my abdomen, becoming a pleasant tingle between my legs, momentarily distracting me from the pain.

This was the first time he had any power over me, and it seemed he liked it.

"I'll be the perfect patient, commodore," I told him, face still on my arms. "But if I hear you being smug about it, I'm unleashing my breasts."

We'd reached a strange truce, an unusual form of mutually assured destruction, but my relationship with Benedict St Stephen was nothing if not unusual.

Doc's painkiller kicked in as the commodore began his stitches. His hand was quick but steady and even, and he talked about his side of the battle as he worked. He was trying to distract me from the pain but I was exhausted and drugged up, so I floated in and out of sleep, tuning in only occasionally to hear about how he marshalled the medic effort and later, his ambush to retake the cannonade.

At long last, he announced he was done, tying off the thread on the last gash, and then gently spreading a cooling ointment across my aching injuries. A sigh of relief escaped me. Sleep, sleep soon.

"Soon," the commodore confirmed, and I suddenly realised I had spoken aloud. "Only the bandages to go. Doc found you some real bandages, instead of the sorry excuse you had before."

There was a long pause.

"Are you going to do it yourself, medic, or do you want me to do it?" My irritation suddenly spiked. "I'm tired, I want to sleep, I'm not in the mood for the games anymore. I have a hell of a mess to clean up later this morning."

"It would be best if I did it. Less chance of you ripping the stitches out straight away." He let a ragged breath.

I rolled my eyes. "Now who's being immature."

"Stand up, please, and put your arms up in front of you." The commodore's voice was brusque and clipped, his military voice.

I did so, my amusement at the situation dampened by the way my legs shook. My breasts were freed from the prison of my arms, metaphorically filling up the room like the proverbial pink elephant.

Luscious, pert, pink elephants.

"Strictly medical purposes," the commodore repeated, as he positioned the bandage and began to wind it around me.

Luscious, pert, strictly-for-medical-purposes pink elephants.

He was standing close behind me, he had to. I could hear him swallow. He wound the bandage around the top of my breasts, without pausing, seeming to focus on ruthless efficiency. Then his hand accidentally brushed against my nipple, immediately bringing it to a point. He froze. His hand hovered there, close enough for the heat from his skin to send shivers across my skin, raising goosebumps across the tender flesh of my breast.

I tell you what, I wasn't thinking about my back anymore.

"Just carry on." I felt impatient, but my voice came out breathy. "The worst has happened, you touched a pirate tit. Get on with it."

"I apologize sincerely." He continued but with his hand now shaking, he bumped and brushed a nipple or the skin at every pass. His breath grew more ragged. I couldn't tell if it was from fear or lust.

"You can pull the bandage a bit tighter than that. They do squish, you know," I told him as he had to recover a slipped loop of bandage. "You've never had to medic a woman before, have you?"

"No." The commodore seemed grateful for the conversation. "Just navy men."

"But you've seen breasts, right?"

"Yes I have." He was gritting his teeth I could tell. He was finally tightening the bandages enough for things to sit stably but without damaging the goods.

"Other than mine? That's tight enough now."

"Other than yours, yes."

"More than one?"

"Seeing as they generally come in a pair, yes." There was a sigh. "All done."

I turned to face my medic. His face was flushed and there was blood on his hands and sleeves. My blood.

"I meant more than one set."

"Stop it, pirate."

"You *have* had sex, haven't you?" The thought suddenly struck me that he might be an actual virgin. I had just assumed he had sex, because everyone on the sea has had sex, it's one of the best ways to pass the time. But maybe the commodore...

"I thought you were tired and in no mood for games." He turned away, plunging his hand into a bowl of already bloody water and scrubbing them with undue vigour.

"That's a no." I grinned, despite the fact I was swaying on my feet.

"It's not a no, it's a non-answer," St Stephen ground out through gritted teeth. He picked up a cloth that was almost clean, either drying his hands or attempting to strangle the offending fabric. "We're done here. Get into bed."

"I'll treasure this memory," I told him, as I turned, "of you ordering me to bed. Truly, it will keep me warm—"

My smart arse comment died on my lips along with my laugh as all the blood rushed out of my head without warning. Up and down became indistinguishable, and grey spots danced in front of my eyes as I collapsed like an unruly drunk taking a cudgel to the head.

Strong hands grabbed me before I kissed the floor of my cabin, wrenching me back to my feet. My back was now against a line of solid warmth. I pressed against it, my only anchor as the cabin spun and pitched around me. Distantly, I heard a voice, but the roaring in my ears drowned it out, a thundering surf and a wild storm only I was experiencing because I had been too cavalier. I had pushed too far and my body was giving me marching orders to be horizontal.

Moments later, the cabin righted itself, and the thundering ceased. The voice came into focus. Commodore St Stephen was telling me to breathe—or perhaps he was talking to himself, since he sounded a little breathless? He was the solid line of warmth at my back, arms holding me tightly against his body to stop me from falling. One arm was across my waist, the other across my torso, hand resting just above my heart —getting a decent handful of boob in the process.

"I'm fine." My voice was barely a croak. "I'm fine."

"You were falling," came his reply, his voice strained.

"Aye, I was."

A heartbeat or ten passed and neither of us moved. The commodore's breathing grew more uneven with each moment. I had no energy for ribaldry anymore. I sank further back against him, breathing in the smell of blood, sweat and sea, and something indescribably masculine that would have made me heady with lust were I not so exhausted.

His hand was still lying against my heart. I put mine over it and pressed it gently against the bandages he had wound there with such deep awkwardness. To my surprise, his hands obliged, fingers curling into the soft flesh of my breast.

Well now.

Now I was the one frozen, entirely surprised as his hand gently cupped a breast, and as his breath whispered across that soft spot where the shoulder becomes neck. Instinctively, I pressed my hips back against him, and as I brushed against something hot and hard in his breeches, the spell was broken. He released me, pulling away so abruptly I nearly fell.

"You should get some sleep, before you pass out." St Stephen brusquely brushed past me, heading for the bed set up for him in the far corner. He climbed in and pulled a blanket over himself without turning to face me once.

Bemused and definitely somewhat aroused, I too dragged myself to my own bed, lying on my front to avoid aggravating the wounds he had so carefully stitched. I smiled to myself. The commodore had hot blood after all.

"You know," I said, breaking the silence, "if you *did* happen to be a virgin, I'm quite happy to help you out with that. You've already met my bosom, my lady's cove is even more impressive. Your cock seemed in favour of it just now."

There was such a long silence I thought he'd either fallen asleep or had resolved to ignore me.

"I'm not a virgin," he finally said in clipped tones. "Now go to sleep."

I did, with a ghost of a smile on my face even after that total clusterfuck of a night.

6

———

My sleep was deep and satisfying. There was no pain in my body, not from my aching muscles, myriad of bruises, or the stitched gashes on my back. My feet did not ache from standing all day and all night, and my head did not pound with exhaustion, dehydration, and fury.

I floated in water that was the exact right temperature, neither too warm nor too cool. It held me gently in its embrace on all sides. It kept me afloat where I was, but there was no pressure to keep my chest from rising and falling softly.

How could I breathe, if I was underwater? I cautiously opened my eyes a slit to take a look, but they were heavy, and I could see nothing but the darkness of the deeps. No mottled sunlight cast its wavery glow here, no light at all to see by. The sailor in me recognised the fathomless deeps of the ocean, the way a religious sort might recognise heaven: the eventual end.

Maybe I was dead? Murdered in my sleep and dumped overboard?

I shrugged, or at least, I shrugged mentally. Worry was too much effort. I felt myself slipping under again, sleep pulling at me like a persistent undertow, and I gave into it. If I was dead, there was no hurry. I'd get where I was going when I got there and I'd probably need my strength to give whoever was there a right bollocking when I met them. So I slept.

Time passed.

I became aware again. I knew it was later, but not how I knew, or how much later. My eyes were still shut, my body still rocked on comfortable tides, and I felt the presence of the Deep around me.

"By rights, she is mine."

The voice came so suddenly I thought my heart would stop. I was glad that sleep still kept my body in its relaxed state otherwise I might have flailed with no grace and sunk like a stone. The voice was so deep I felt it rather than heard it. In my mind I saw cliff faces with caves hollowed by the sea over decades, the sway of the tides over the ocean floor, the gravel-like crunch of rocks, ships and other debris sliding against rock. Back and forth, back and forth. The voice was bottomless, it was ageless, it was pitiless.

I'm not gonna lie, if I was awake, I'd have probably pissed myself.

I was so busy thinking about that, I almost missed the reply.

"You know you step out of bounds." The voice was human sized, masculine and it made me think of wind ruffling shining brown hair. "I drew on your power, not her. The debt is owed by me."

"*I* step out of bounds?" Its laughter was a hull cracking in a storm. "My blessing was wielded by a petty human sailor for a petty human squabble, because *you* thought it fitting, and *you* say that I step out of line! Shall the seal call the shark to order now, and the krill have words to the whale?"

"I am not a seal. I did not upset the nature of things." The voice sounded so familiar, but I couldn't place it. I struggled to open my eyes but something primal in me kept them shut. There was something I shouldn't see, my gut insisted. I wasn't supposed to be here.

"It upsets the nature of things for a human to wield my power," the voice repeated, forcefully, breakers crashing on jagged rocks, a place with no hope for making landfall.

"It is the nature of things for me to draw on that power and last night it did more good in her hands than in mine."

"What *good* did it do? Ships were reduced to kindling. Sailors sank into the deep. The outcome was the same."

"*Not for the people.*" That fierceness, that protectiveness. I'd felt it before. It was at the edge of my memory. I scrabbled for it but it disappeared, pulled back by a tide of thoughts.

"People." Now the voice was as placid and dangerous as a riptide dragging the unwary swimmer out to sea. "What do I care for the people? Sailors and ships sink to the deep: English, French, Spanish, Dutch, pirate, navy, passenger, cook. Their bones all look the same lying on the ocean floor."

It was probably a good thing I couldn't talk or I'd tell this thing to fuck all the way off. At least, that's what I told myself. My physical body was still as perfectly comfortable as it had been before but my internal knees were quaking and my internal teeth were chattering.

"If it doesn't matter to you who ends up in the deeps," the human voice argued, "then it shouldn't matter if I meddle. I'll pay off my debt for drawing your power. Leave Captain Flint out of it."

Wait, wait, wait, this sounded important. I'd have bet my

ship that the human wielding power last night was one of the Grimsteads, but it had been me? News to me. Whatever it was, I didn't remember it being much use. Who was the human? Was it bloody Lysander? It didn't sound like him, but he was the one with the history of fucking about in dreams. I put all my efforts into dragging my eyelids open.

Open your eyes. Open your eyes.

"You've marked her as one of ours. She wears that debt on her skin and on her soul."

"She will not be yours!" the human voice all but bellowed.

My eyes opened just enough to see. Underwater. Glimpses of rotting boards and loose ropes. A shipwreck?

The man. His face. His hair. His voice.

"Sebastian?" I thought I had whispered but my voice echoed around us though I had shouted.

He looked at me, features frozen in horror, opening his mouth to speak.

If he said something I never heard it, because I saw what he was talking to. Horror welled up in me, so potent that escape wasn't even an option.

"You *are* annoying," it said, and made a flicking motion. I felt myself hurtle backward into blackness, as though rushed off my feet by a rogue wave crashing over the deck, back into the recesses of deepest sleep, my mind desperate to leave the horrific form of the huge voice of the deeps behind.

7

I woke to the sound of hammering on my cabin door.

"Captain Flint, you're needed." It was Ginger.

I squinted at the sunshine pouring through the closed curtains over the cabin windows. It was a few hours before we were to sail. Time for me to be on deck. I glanced over at the commodore's bed, but it was already empty. Fucking over-achiever.

"Aye, Ginger. Give a soul a minute for a stiff drink," I called out, which sounded far better than what I really needed: a minute to shake the sand from my brain. I blinked in the sunlight, vaguely recalling a nightmare where two people were bargaining over me. The details slipped from me the harder I tried to catch them, leaving me dizzy and disoriented.

"Fuck it." I swung my legs out of bed, and hunted around for a clean (or at least, not blood soaked) shirt and boots. I didn't bother doing anything about my hair. It was still in the braid I'd put it in before battle and it would take a miracle to brush it out. I wasn't about to rip my stitches open on account of my hair. No, I would save that inevitable eventuality for when I made a daring escape, had a stylish duel, or (fingers crossed) had really wild sex with one or more attractive men.

I really hoped it would be the latter.

I took a quick swig of rum to get my brain juices flowing. I had a lot of work to do first—. starting with the bratty magician.

I strode over the cage and whipped off its cover, revealing a shirtless Lysander, curled up and snoring softly. He'd managed to get out of his gag, and now his head lolled to one side. He had drooled while he slept.

Not that I was going to tell him, but it was kind of adorable.

Instead, I slapped my hand on top of the cage, rattling the entire contraption and jolting the sleeping wizard awake.

"Rise and shine, Grimstead." I unlocked the side panel of the cage while he made distinctly unimpressive snorting noises as he woke up. "Time to get to work."

"What is this?" He eyed the now-open cage with distrust.

"You're using your magic to help make the ship go faster, remember? Can't do that from a cage. You need robes and chalk and a box fort." I gesticulated vaguely. I was pretty sure he only needed the chalk but there was no law that said I couldn't tease him—and if there was, I'd break it anyway.

"I didn't agree to that." Lysander's posh boy accent danced the line between whining and disdain. He slowly unfolded himself from his prison, stretching out his limbs. "I said I wouldn't make the ship go slower."

I waited for him to finish uncricking his neck before I stepped in close.

"So you wanna go back in the cage?" I asked, almost nose to nose with him, my gaze boring into his cobalt eyes. I loved negotiating with people who were the same height as me. "The way I see it, if you make the ship go fast, you're one of the most important people on board. If you're just a risk of sabotage, then..." I trailed off with a smile. A smile that showed a lot of teeth.

"It *is* in my interest to get to Port Elizabeth as soon as possible," Lysander said after a second. He tilted his head, our eyes still fixed on each other. "You did promise, though..." His eyes drifted down across my body.

I leaned in closer, putting my mouth to his ear, and he ran a hand over my hip. "Don't worry, I'll play with you before I put you away for the night." I whispered. I felt his pulse speed up. I bit his ear, making him yelp. "I hope you're ready. I'm quite a handful."

He grabbed my wrist as I turned away. I turned back, irritated, but what I saw stopped me. His other hand was gently rubbing his ear, and his blue eyes burned with a fire I had only seen glimpses of before. "As always, Flint, you've underestimated me."

"I hope so." I put as much bravado in my voice as I could muster. "Right now you're as appealing as a dead fish. But there's a whole day for you to impress me. Get dressed and head up to the helm. If you go missing, I'll find you and feed you your own dick, and it won't be any fun, do you hear me?"

I strode out, heart pounding from unexpected sexual tension, leaving Lysander muttering darkly behind me.

8

It was a beautiful day in the Caribbean and the Last Doubloon was a hive of activity. The sun was bright but it wasn't stinking hot (yet), the sky was a cloudless blue, the palm trees swayed and the only thing that ruined this idyllic little image was that the tranquil island breeze stank of blood, flesh, gunpowder and sweat.

At least I wasn't one of the poor bastards floating face-down in the harbour with seagulls pecking at my back. They wouldn't be there for long. The dead bastards in the sea were being fought over the large contingent of sharks that had turned up to feast. The town's clean up crew was out in force too. A small team of girls deftly manoeuvred the dead that washed up on the beach onto rickety carts. They were chattering cheerfully while they worked. One of them waved to me. I waved back.

It's important to love your work.

I stepped off the dock onto solid land. All around me, the non-combatants had come out of the woodwork to deal with the dead, the injured, and the drunk survivors. I shielded my eyes from the sun and saw one of the grounded Haddrick and Mercer ships being crawled over by pirates. The pile of weapons and valuables on the deck grew larger by the second.

"Good morning, captain." Sebastian walked up beside me, a sheaf of papers in hand, and Dauntless on his shoulder.

"I heard tell of a type of flesh eating fish that lives in rivers, in that jungle south of the Caribbean," I said, still watching the pirates strip the ship. "They say if a donkey falls in the water, a swarm of those fuckers turns up, each only a few inches big, but they strip that donkey to bones in seconds."

"Pirhanas," the commodore said. I hadn't recognised him next to Sebastian. With his beard getting longer and clothes getting worn, he was looking more pirate-like by the minute. "Vicious, dangerous creatures."

We watched the Haddrick and Mercer ship's valuables get carted onto land by a swarm of industrious and determined thieves.

"Sure," I said with an easy grin. "But you can't deny they're fucking cool."

The commodore pressed his mouth into a thin line and didn't answer. Dauntless shrieked a couple of times, perhaps his version of a laugh in the parrot form. He flapped his massive red wings a few times, landing on my shoulder.

"Captain, I hope you don't mind, but in the absence of your first mate, I've temporarily assumed the duties of making ready for sail." Sebastian held out the papers. "I hope it was not out of order. The commodore said you had... not gotten to bed until quite a late hour, which he takes full responsibility for."

Dauntless shrieked his name several times, right by my ear, causing me to very nearly lose control of my bladder. Which of course would have meant I'd have to kill all witnesses. While the commodore was no real loss, I did rather like Sebastian.

"Shriek in my ear again," I told the bird, "and I'll nail your beak shut. If you shit on my shirt, I'll roast you for dinner. Are we clear?"

The parrot indignantly ruffled its feathers, which I took for agreement.

"You need not worry about her honour, Dauntless," the commodore said with ridiculous solemnity to the parrot on my shoulder. He was almost as red as the feathers. "I was performing medical aid and she was a difficult patient."

"I do whatever I want with my honour. Neither you nor the parrot get a say in it." I grabbed the papers out of Sebastian's hand, and looked at them. Val's neat handwriting had been annotated by an elegant script. My vision swam. I rubbed my eyes. I swear I'm smart, I know how to outfit my own ship, but deciphering Val's logistical arrangements was like playing chess with a Russian.

"You keep doing that, Sebastian. Dauntless, stick with him, and make sure he doesn't do anything I wouldn't like." I pushed the papers back at Sebastian. As my hand touched his chest, the sun, sky and sea faded into grey around me. I was in darkness, beneath fathomless depths.

"Captain?" came a voice from the darkness. I blinked. Sebastian peered at me, dark eyes framed by a fan of long hair that was impossibly perfect for the morning after a battle. "Are you all right?"

Fragments of dream floated to the surface of my mind. There had been a terrible voice and a human voice.

"It was you." I yanked my hand back from Sebastian. "I had a dream about you."

"Was it anything good?" he asked, his tone light, lips curling into a smile that didn't quite reach his eyes.

"No. It was more like a nightmare." I shook my head. "I don't remember."

"Sounds like the work of Grimstead," the commodore said. "Nightmares have been his stock and trade this whole journey."

"Obviously." It hadn't even occurred to me. "I'll deal with it later. First I have a crew to find. Sebastian, carry on with the resupply."

As I strode past him, Sebastian caught my hand. "I don't know what dream you had, captain," he said softly, his warm breath making me shiver, "or whatever frightening things happened in it, but I'm sorry I was a part of it. I swear by Davy Jones' locker, I would never put you in harm's way."

It would have been a very romantic moment—if my ex-boyfriend the parrot hadn't started flapping his wings and cawing loudly.

"I'm sure it was just too many painkillers and wizardry for one night, or as the commodore said, that weasel magician trying his hand again." I gestured at his papers. "Have us ready by the noon tide."

Sebastian nodded and returned to resupply, moving in and around the clean up.

"Commodore, you're with me," I said. "We're tracking down the crew."

"Why don't you go track down your crew, and I'll help Sebastian with the resupply?"

"I'm hurt, I thought you liked me. You seemed to like me last night."

"Do you even pay attention to what you say, or do you spout ribaldry like a sex-starved fountain?"

"Well, fuck you."

"You've certainly been trying your best." He grabbed my arm, not forcefully, but enough to stop me in my tracks. "Flint, for god's sake just listen to me for one minute, then you can go back to being a giant pain in the ass."

"What?" I pulled free, and crossed my arms, trying not to wince as the motion pulled my stitches.

"Sebastian vanished last night." St Stephen lowered his voice, his head bent close to my own. "After Val was taken, he was helping pull people from the water, until his boat turned up empty. They thought he'd drowned."

"Obviously he didn't."

"A few hours later, he comes strolling up the beach like he'd been for a swim."

"Maybe he had been. Have you been listening to the gossip of drunk pirates? I thought you were way too smart for that shit."

"Look at him. And look at me. He doesn't look like he's had a swim, let alone participated in a naval battle."

"Are you jealous?"

"No!" He almost hissed in frustration. "I'm going to pretend you're smart, Magpie. We don't know who our enemies are or who is working for them. Whatever fire you have in your loins for Sebastian, I suggest you sit on some ice, because you need to use your brain."

"Because he looks well-groomed and some drunk pirates said he vanished?"

St Stephen's pale blue eyes, far greyer than Lysander's, glittered with a hard edge. "Because look how suddenly and without conflict he took over running your ship."

That landed like a gut punch.

Before I could muster a response, a scrawny youth of indeterminate gender came barrelling up to me. "Captain Flint. Gunnarson and the captains are meeting in an hour. They want you there."

9

———

Gunnarson gave the impression of being short even though he was taller than me. This was due to the fact his shoulders were so broad he almost formed a square. His blond hair and beard were woven into intricate braids and decorated with beads and gemstones. People better traveled than me told me his unusual accent was from the northern part of Europe, where it gets so cold that your tits and bollocks freeze off unless you wear a whole bear for a cape. Which probably explained why Gunnarson claimed descent from the old Vikings, Europe's original pirates. I once heard a pirate question this claim, which Gunnarson rebutted by smashing the doubter's shin with a massive hammer.

All of which is to say, Gunnarson is a heavyweight on the seas and I'm not just talking about that ridiculous hammer.

The captains who'd arrived for this little parley were crowded into a room above the tavern designed for just such a purpose. The table in the middle was round and heavily scarred with marks of weapons and the stains of liquor and blood. There weren't enough chairs so the latecomers were forced to sit on barrels or lean against the walls.

The tension in the air was somewhat mitigated by the blue skies out the open shutters and the music down below, made by some folks who were clearly damn grateful to have survived the night.

"You got a mate coming, Flint?" Gunnarson asked, after taking a mental register of who was in the room. Every captain had brought a first or other trusted mate with them. I brought Dauntless.

"Just the parrot." I leaned back in my chair, trying not to wince at the pressure on the wounds, or let myself get distracted by the memories of the commodore it conjured up.

"Flint, this isn't a joke. You know the protocol." Gunnarson looked as serious as a snake bite.

"I do know the protocol, Gunnar, but my first mate got kidnapped last night, and my other trusted mates are dealing with my prisoners or taking the lead on the resupply." I sighed and spread my hands. "You're gonna have to make do with just me."

Gunnarson gave me a level look.

It dawned on me that he wasn't threatening me. He was trying to help. Having a mate was insurance, back up. I was swimming in shark infested waters and I brought a bird to help me. I couldn't very well explain that the bird was Captain Dauntless without them never taking me seriously again.

I felt a lot better about this meeting knowing Gunnarson wasn't out to get me. I returned his level gaze, and he shrugged.

"What about your navy lad? Ben?" someone asked. "I know he's new on your crew and all but he's got potential, mark me words. He'll be captaining on his own before you know it."

There were murmurs of agreement from the sailors in the room.

"He saved dozens of lives last night, organising to fish folks out of the water like he did," Camilla Lopez, captain of a former Spanish galleon, said.

"And the way he led the cannonade ambush!"

"Yes, yes, he's very good," I snapped. "I'll convey the commendations of the captains to him. Can we move on to business before we miss the tide? I don't want to waste time getting to Port Elizabeth." I also did not want to sit here and listen to a bunch of pirates unknowingly worship Commodore St Stephen. Dauntless made a low, repeated chirping noise in my ear. I'd bet my ship it was laughter.

"Three matters to deal with, the way I see it," Gunnarson said, leaning back in his chair. It creaked. "The matter of the spoils, the matter of the prisoners, and the matter of the kidnapping."

"There's no *matter* with the kidnapping." I crossed my arms. "I'm going to handle it. I'm going to go to Port Elizabeth, and—"

"Shut up, Captain Flint." Gunnarson's fist pounded the scarred table. "None of this is your matter anymore. Your fucking trouble has us all caught up in it like fish in nets."

I fell silent, more out of shock than anything.

Murmurs of agreement circled the room. I stared ahead while Gunnarson moved the topic back to the first issue, that of spoils. I tuned out while the captains negotiated, not much caring for whatever pittance would come to me from the scraps salvaged off the brute force ships of Haddrick and Mercer. All I wanted was to leave and get ready to sail.

"Captain Flint, do you agree to the split of the spoils?" Gunnarson's voice brought me back.

"Aye, I agree."

Then we discussed the prisoners. Several captains had talked to the captains of the captured Haddrick and Mercer ships, and were shocked to find that most of the sailors on board were women.

"That definitely wasn't the case when I was on Wilfred Haddrick's flagship, I can promise you that," I said. "Wall to wall sausage fest."

The Dutch captain, Johannes, spoke. "Regardless, his cannon meat ranks seem to be filled with women who have complicated contracts, from what I have been able to understand. Which is little." He shrugged.

"A load of shite, Johannes, and ye know it," boomed Mac, with their Scottish bur. "Ye speak better English than most of us, at leastways when it comes to legal shite. Don't be a cock, jus' tell us what the rub is."

"You haggis eating prick." Johannes flicked his one good eye over at Mac, but relented. "Their families are collateral against their service. If their service is not completed then their family must pick it up. Since in almost every case family means children, the delay between when the original person holding the contract ceases to be able to carry out their duties and the next family member being able to pick up service is years, that time is added onto the remaining time in the contract."

"That's bullshit!" I shouted. Every other pirate in the room shouted curse words of their preference or in their own first language. Dauntless shrieked. "Why the fuck did they agree to it? Are they stupid?"

"Desperation. Mostly widows," Camilla Lopez said. "Navy

46

widows. The navy doesn't offer much by way of recompense if your husband dies at sea, and they don't hire you if you don't have a dick. And of course, the promise of revenge is alluring." Her dark eyes flashed at me. "A lot of them seem to think you sank their husband's ship, Flint."

An incredulous laugh escaped me. "I'm flattered, but there's no profit and a world of hurt in sinking navy ships. I haven't even come close to sinking a navy ship in years."

Captain Lopez shrugged her shoulders, her collection of saint's emblems around her neck jingling lightly. "Si, but it is an effective recruitment tactic. Not *all* of them are after your blood, Flint. Some of them just hate all of us in general."

"Well thank fuck for that," Mac's first mate said. "I was getting jealous at all the hate boners that Flint is getting."

"Mate, if I could give them all to you, I would." I spread my arms. "What are we going to do with them?"

A brief, heated exchange followed. Several pirates, led by Johannes, argued for their immediate execution. Most others thought that was a waste of bullets and in my case, would stir up worse blood than was necessary. It was agreed they'd be kept here and their officers taken for ransoming.

"That just leaves your mission, Flint," Gunnarson said. "And we have more than a few questions we want answers to."

I slammed all four legs of my chair back onto the ground.

"You're going to absolutely hate the answer to all of them." I held up my hand before anyone could get a word out. "It was magic. Fucking wizardry. The real deal. Ships zipping around with no wind? Magic. Cannon balls dropping out of the air? Magic. Blinding light column that whisked away Val? Magic." I spread my hands and grimaced at the roomful of stony faces staring at me. "Told you you weren't going to like it."

"You're fucking with us." Johannes' leaned in so close I could smell his rancid breath. "You in league with them? Playing a trick?"

"We all know I've never planned that far ahead in my life, you tulip smuggling prick." I stared him in his good eye, trying not to flinch at the nasty scar over the other one.

"Let her talk. Flint, tell us more." Captain Lopez ran her fingers over her saints emblems.

I told them everything I knew, which wasn't much, and sounded mad enough as it was. The only thing I left out was the bit about the parrot.

"Look, in the end it doesn't matter what you think." I shrugged. "I have the commodore, I have Lysander Grimstead and I have my own self and I'll be taking all three of us to Port Elizabeth. Who's going to stop me?"

"Flint, lass, we *can* just kill ye now and take yer ship and prisoners and corpse and deliver it to them." Mac squinted at me. "Did ye take a head blow in the fighting last night?"

"That's big of you, Mac, truly. Walking into an obvious trap like that for me. Right into Port Elizabeth." I stood up. "When do we go? Are we taking your ship or mine?"

Mac hesitated and exchanged looks with the other captains.

"She's got a point," Gunnarson boomed.

"She's either right or she's mad," Eduardo, Camilla Lopez's twin brother and first mate said, with a melodious Spanish accent. His sister nodded.

"Neither is good."

"Let Flint go. She's as wily as Loki ever was." Gunnarson slammed his tankard down. "You bastards can get your own selves armed while she risks her neck. I don't see why you are complaining. If she dies, then one of us can be the next famous one. I say it should be Johannes."

Johannes swore at him in Dutch and they all agreed that it was in fact a fine idea that I go, on my own, into a probable trap while they stayed behind to deal with the hostages, defend the Last Doubloon or whatever it is they wanted to do.

You gotta love pirates. Always looking out for number one.

10

___

A dozen pirate captains and their loyal mates poured out of the room, our pent up energy spilling into the open. No one stayed for convivial conversation. We all had our headings set, and it was time to get going. Anyone who says pirates are lazy hasn't met any. The only way to get a pirate to stay still is to get them falling down drunk, nail their feet to the deck or to kill them. Otherwise, there's always something we've got to be doing.

Fired up by the meeting, I charged back to the ship. Dauntless spread his wings and flew ahead to the ship. He was perched on a deck railing when I got on board.

"Yeah, you win, but wings are cheating," I called to him. He ruffled his feathers in a distinctly smug way. I shook my head and took stock of the situation on board.

My new recruits were loading themselves and whatever possessions they were bringing to sea onto the boat. Plenty of pirates at a loose end and with an axe to grind: I had my pick of sailors before the captains meeting. No disrespect to Val's people, who were competent enough on the seas, but it made me feel better to top up the crew with hands that spent most of their time hauling ropes and firing cannons, rather than, you know, *firing cannons.*

Peggy ambled past me, balancing a load of long wooden beams, managing better on her pair of peg legs than I could on my sea legs.

"What's that then?" I asked.

She gave me a devious smile. "I'm stealing one of the ballistas."

"Well. That's all right then." I waved her on. "As you were, mate." I didn't know if a ballista could work on a ship but if anyone could make it work, it was Peggy and the deck minnows.

Sharky saluted me as he galloped on board, grinning ear to ear. "Aye aye, captain!" He beamed. "Sailing with Captain Flint. It's a dream come true."

"Lad, are you sure about this?" I crossed my arms and regarded the green young man in front of me. "You're sailing with the most wanted face in the Caribbean. I'm sailing into a British stronghold, into what is certainly a trap, with only my cunning as my compass. We'll most likely die."

"I'm going to sail with the most wanted face in the Caribbean to make the most daring rescue in pirate history or go down to Davy Jones' locker with one hell of a story." He saluted again. "I won't let you down, Cap'n."

"Aye lad, you're the right sort of madman for this. But stop with the saluting, this ain't the navy." Sharky stopped himself halfway through a salute and ran off so fast he skidded on the newly cleaned deck.

I love an enthusiastic recruit. I hope I didn't get him killed.

"He seems enamoured with you." Sebastian's voice came from beside me.

"It's just the air of danger," I told him. "The young pirates all go hard or wet at the prospect of near death."

Sebastian laughed, the sound traveling down my spine like a caress. His white shirt provided a beautiful contrast to his tan, and I couldn't help but follow all the lines of his body up to his very kissable lips.

"I've completed all the necessary tasks for setting off," those kissable lips were saying, the mundanity of the words jerking me back to the moment. Sebastian offered me papers covered in notes and sums. I'd have to go over those later, when I didn't have a ship to sail and no one was trying to kill me. Funny how moments like that were getting difficult to come by.

"Thanks." The commodore's warnings about Sebastian bubbled up inside me as uncomfortable suspicion. "How'd you pick it up so fast?"

"I've worked with Val for a few years." He looked mildly surprised at the question. "She's very organised, as you know." I nodded. "I asked after you, but Doc said you'd been injured and weren't to be woken yet, so I found the notes and completed the things Val had begun. I've written down any changes I had to make. With so many ships setting out, supply negotiations became trickier."

I nodded along mutely, feeling a little silly. "You're not angling for first mate or something?" I asked, with my usual level of diplomacy.

Sebastian's eyebrows hiked up, nearly disappearing into his lovely hair. "I'm not. I don't care for rank, and if I can be honest..." He shrugged. "I wouldn't be on the ocean if Val hadn't asked me to come. I prefer to stay on land."

My disgust at this idea was obviously written all over my face, because Sebastian laughed.

"Blasphemy?"

"It's a damn crime is what it is. You're one of the best sailors I've met!" He was currently one of two people I trusted at the wheel other than myself, and the other guy was only there because I wanted a sliver of time when neither Sebastian nor I were steering the ship. Theoretically, we could just fuck up against the helm, but I'm not that much of an exhibitionist.

I took a deep breath before I spoke again. "You don't have to sail anymore. If you'd rather stay on the island."

"Magpie." He tilted his head slightly, making me think he was coming in for a kiss, but he stopped at a polite distance. "Just like you, I can't leave Val in trouble like that. And, if I may be honest…" His eyes darkened slightly as he leaned in to whisper in my ear. "I'm determined to keep you awake one of these nights. You've fallen asleep on me twice. It's not going to happen a third time."

My entire body broke out in goosebumps, and warmth pooled in my nether regions, as I remembered Sebastian's hands in the dark.

"Part of your official duty, then, is to keep me awake every night until Port Elizabeth," I told him. "But right now, I need you to go and take over from Doc in the hold. They've been awake all night. I checked in earlier and Elspeth still needs to be watched—" that bitch always needed to be watched, as far as I was concerned and not just medically "—but Doc needs to sleep. I can't send the commodore, he might slit her throat."

"We can't be losing our fearless moral compass, can we," Sebastian jested.

I stepped away from him, telling my strained body to hold it together for a little longer. As I turned to give orders to prepare for cast off, a very different kind of shudder passed through me, like a chill current in warm waters.

It had *definitely* been Sebastian in my nightmare. My gut said there was more to it than the just usual rum-fueled rubbish that my brain threw at me in my sleeping hours.

11

———————

Sailing out of the Last Doubloon, past the silent cannonade and hitting the open waters, a world of worry dropped from my shoulders.

I'd been on land for barely a day, and it had felt like a month. A really terrible month. There's too much to think about on land, I reflected, standing at the helm with my hair whipping behind me, looking out at the clear blue sky and deeper blue of the ocean. There were too many directions things could come at you from. Out here, on the fathomless deeps, all my problems were in one place, and I could throw them overboard anytime I wanted.

Well, most of my problems were in one place. The rest were in Port Elizabeth, a place I never thought I'd ever see, and if I did, I certainly wouldn't be heading there of my own volition.

More's the pity for Port Elizabeth.

"Are you always this feral when sailing, or is that what you look like when you have to think?"

Lysander Grimstead leaned against a mast smirking at me.

I realised I was baring my teeth. "Just thinking about how much of Port Elizabeth I can blow to the bottom of the sea," I replied, taking one hand off the wheel to give him the finger.

The bottom of the sea.

"Speaking of which," I continued, facing him. "I know you fucked with my dreams again last night."

Lysander's pale eyebrows shot up. "You can't blame all your bad dreams on me, captain. Whatever you dreamt last night, it was all you." He shrugged elegantly and spread his hands. "I'm out of the nightmare business."

He'd found a cerulean shirt somewhere, tied around the waist with a black scarf. The vibrant blue made his cobalt blue eyes stand out against his pale skin. The only thing marring the elegance was the black and purple bruising around the eye where I'd punched him last night and lines of tiredness around his eyes and mouth.

I was glad I wasn't the only one looking worse for wear.

"Yeah, you'd say that, wouldn't you." My retort lacked conviction. I'd seen the surprise on his face. Somehow the thought that Lysander wasn't behind whatever unsettling dream had haunted me in the night was worse than thinking he was. Better the devil you know, or something like that.

"I was asleep," Lysander said after a moment. "It took me about five minutes to get that gag out. After that I passed out until you woke me. If I had a choice about matters, and I wasn't worried about getting my throat cut, I'd be sleeping now."

"We're not gonna cut your throat," I reminded him. "You're tied to the ship, so you say, and besides, we need you for the ransom."

"As if any of that matters, when you don't think about repercussions." Lysander smirked again. "Killing me would certainly fuck you all well and proper, but I'd still be dead. Or worse, stuck haunting a sunken ship."

I shuddered. The thought of being alone in the depths of the ocean struck a fear in me. That was new. It was an occupational hazard as a pirate, and it had never worried me before.

I did what I do best: shoved it out of my head for Later Magpie to deal with.

"Can't believe you slept in that fucking cage," I said, either to irritate him or move the conversation along, even I wasn't sure.

"I'm certain you wanted me awake and miserable, but you failed to take some things into consideration." He was suddenly right behind me, his hands folding over mine on the captain's wheel. "*I have a body.* For the first time in over a year."

His long locks fell against my cheeks even as his breath brushed against my neck.

Trying to throw him off, or kick him, would wrench us off course.

"You're going to get kicked in the balls for the first time in over a year if you don't back the fuck off," I growled, hoping he wouldn't realise it was an empty threat.

Mercifully, he stepped away, and stood beside me instead. "You don't have any idea how exhausting sorcery is, so I'll forgive you for not knowing."

"You're a pompous prick, you know that?"

He kept talking like he hadn't heard. "But having a body for the first time in a year, doing that much sorcery, the adrenaline of the battle... I was exhausted. I ought to thank you for interrupting my liaison with those two fine residents of that pirate bolt hole. I would have likely humiliated myself by falling asleep the second I got horizontal. You're aware of what that's like, I know."

"Are you looking to even up your eyes?" I asked him. "Maybe I can't throw you overboard but I can get you a matching pair of black eyes without a problem."

Lysander shut his eyes rather than reply. A few seconds later, the ship shuddered, and several crew lost their footing on deck. The previously full sails began to slacken and the ship started to slow.

Smith started barking orders to the crew on the sails. The wind blew my hair back again, but the sails continued to slacken.

"I can stop your ship dead in the water," Lysander said from beside me. The edges of his eyes and mouth were pinched, and his breathing was ragged. The effort of holding the ship against the ocean was costing him.

"*You*—" I stepped away from the wheel. Hatred surged through me and it took every ounce of self control I possessed to not punch him again. I flexed my hands impotently, and clenched my teeth as a red mist settled around the edges of my vision.

"You just have to be nice, that's all." Despite the strain, he managed to look smug.

"Are all sorcerers dicks or is that just a special Grimstead family trait?" I asked, somehow forming coherent words, as I stepped out of range of bodily violence.

"I put up with you pushing me around last night because I was exhausted. The violence, the abuse you subjected me to, it stops now, Flint. You need me. And I'm very good at being an uncooperative prick." He smiled tightly. "I make a much better friend than enemy. We've got that much in common."

"And nothing else," I ground out from behind gritted teeth.

"Are you going to be nice now?"

"I've never been nice in my life. Ask anybody."

"In lieu of nice I'll settle for you not laying an unwanted hand on my person again. Just treat me like I'm a part of your ship. Which I am."

Before I could think of a scathing retort, a cry came from the crow's nest.

"Sails! Sails port side! Three ships and they're flying navy colours!"

12

———

"Find me the commodore!" I bellowed as I pulled out my ship's glass. Scanning the horizon on the port side, I quickly found the sails. Three ships, navy colours. My lookout hadn't been mistaken. Their current heading indicated we would cross paths. We had no choice but to engage.

"I can get us past them," Lysander said. "We wouldn't need much speed. They won't be expecting it. We can just speed ahead before they get into cannon range."

"Can't," I said tersely, lowering the glass from my eye. "That'd make us a very noticeable target."

Benedict St Stephen bounded up to the top deck, out of breath and sweaty. Whatever he'd been doing, he'd obviously been hard at work. I approved.

"Sails?" he asked, between breaths.

I passed him the glass and pointed. "Three navy vessels. What can you tell us?"

"It's hard to say. Whether or not they engage depends on what their orders are."

"See? We should run," Lysander chimed in again.

I spared him a glance. He looked nervous. A healthy reaction to the prospect of a firefight with the navy. "Get your chalk and robes, wizard boy," I told him, and he fled with obvious relief.

Judith bustled onto the deck with all her bags. "What can I do?" she asked breathlessly.

I waved at her to pipe down. "We're flying Haddrick and Mercer colours. They should think we're good law-abiding traders. Right?" I looked at the commodore. "The whole point of being a law abiding commercial entity is that you don't get bothered by the navy?"

"Depends how much you bribe the navy." Lysander returned with a large book under his arm and a pouch of what I presumed were magical... bits.

"The navy can't be bribed," the commodore ground out.

"*You* can't be bribed," Sebastian said. "I've met navy men with far less scruples than some pirates."

That was a fascinating revelation about Sebastian, but we didn't have time to dwell on it.

"They're not adjusting course," the commodore said. "I don't believe we're under threat. I'm not sure where they are headed, but they don't appear to be interested in us."

"Could they be going for the Last Doubloon?" I asked. "They can't repulse a naval attack, not after last night. We need to stop them."

"Doubtful the navy would send three vessels to deal with that port, especially if they were informed about the port by Haddrick and Mercer." Commodore St Stephen looked up at me from the ship's glass. "Your fervour is admirable, but the Last Doubloon is better equipped to handle their own defense than we are. The cannonade is functional and there are still several defense capable crews there. You, however, have been entrusted with an important errand. I strongly suggest you focus on it."

Judith's mouth turned into a little 'o' of surprise and she took a large step back. I opened my mouth and shut it again. His tone had not been patronising, but his words stung all the more because he was right. I had an important job, and I had gotten distracted. It shouldn't take the fucking commodore of the navy to tell me what my business was.

Also, I should most definitely not be getting all warm inside at being called *admirable* by the commodore.

"Fine," I snapped, snatching the glass back from him. "But if so much as a single person dies back at the Doubloon because you told me to let these navy jerks pass, it's on your head."

"I'll try to live with the pirate deaths on my conscience," he replied dryly.

Nothing to do then but sail on tensely, watching the navy ships draw closer until we could see them with our naked eyes. When we passed each other, everyone on deck was under instruction to be as busy as possible so as not to be more than blurs of moving bodies. The wind was good, and the navy ships gave us a reasonably wide berth. As they passed us and began to recede into the distance several hours later the ship let out a collective breath of relief.

I waited until the sun had set before calling a strategy meeting in my cabin. By that time, we were sufficiently clear of the navy ships that everyone was back to normal, had eaten dinner and those who weren't on night shift had had a few drinks. Most importantly, Dauntless was back in his human form and I wouldn't have to decipher his irritating squawks—his irritating words would be plain enough. I left Whiskey Pete on the helm—an Irishman named for his smuggling runs, rather than for his frequent inebriation (before anyone calls me completely reckless) - and joined the crowd.

My strategic committee consisted of Edward Dauntless (helping himself to a late dinner), Lysander, Sebastian, the commodore, Judith, and Smith, who had been a long serving member of Dauntless's crew before Elspeth had sunk said ship. Smith had not seen Dauntless in the battle the previous night and was currently torn between disbelief and outrage at his former captain for not telling him he was alive.

I surveyed the ragtag collection of individuals and reminded myself it was the sea's finest, only missing Val, who was the smartest of the lot of us.

"Where've ye been hiding?" Smith bellowed, then visibly tried to reign himself in. "Sorry, captain, it's just—by Neptune's hairy arse, why didn't ye tell us?"

"Don't talk to me like that. I'm your captain." Despite his haughty words, Dauntless wouldn't meet Smith's eyes.

"Not here on this boat ye ain't." Smith's nostrils flared. "I'm old enough to be yer father. See if I'm not strong enough to bend ye over my knee and—"

"Smith," I interrupted the older man. "What Dauntless isn't telling you is that during the day he's a parrot."

The older pirate sputtered.

"Magpie," Dauntless growled, a sound that would have been formidable, if he didn't have his mouth full of mashed potato at the time.

"Smith is one of your most loyal mates. I don't care what you tell the rest of the crew out there, you can tell them you're a rum induced hallucination for all I care, but Smith deserves the truth." I threw myself in the last remaining chair at the table that Sebastian had kept open for me—so many reasons to like that man, I swear. I poured myself a half tankard of decent rum and took a swig. "In fact, I want the truth from everyone in here. I know our business is being shady as fuck, but we need to be on the same page if we're going to pull off this mission."

I got a murmur of agreements, aye-ayes, yesses and nods. Most of them were even telling the truth.

"Why are we all here?" Lysander lounged on the decorative pouf that the commodore had sewn me up on last night.

"Glad you asked." I had cleared the table before the meeting, relocating my pile of clutter onto the floor so I could lay out a map. Who says I'm not organised? "We're two days clear sailing away from Port Elizabeth. Commodore, is the navy presence likely to get worse the closer we get?"

Commodore St Stephen pressed his lips into a thin line and hesitated several seconds before answering. "Yes. There are patrols along here, here, and here." He traced several lines on the map. "Evading them is out of the question. Even if we dodge the outer patrols, we can't progress through *here* without being questioned, or engaging in a firefight."

"Can we win a firefight?" I asked.

"Every navy ship has twice the firepower of *The Queen's Liberty*, if not more."

"And if we stopped and talked to them, they would almost certainly clap me in irons along with everyone else on board, putting a neat stop to all of this?" I gestured widely.

"Without doubt, yes," the commodore confirmed.

"But if we were a *navy* ship, escorting the survivors of a pirate attack..." I trailed off and grinned.

Everyone stared at me in confusion, except Dauntless who immediately caught on and started laughing.

"Aye, that'd probably work, captain, but we don't look like a navy ship," Smith offered. "How were ye planning to bamboozle them?"

"Easy. We just rob one of these other navy ships and take their clothes and colours."

"I beg your—" The commodore spluttered. "No. No, we will not be doing that. I won't have any part of it."

"That's fine, you can be in the brig for that bit." I grinned maniacally. I loved a good plan and I knew in my gut I had a good plan. "I only need you for the bit where we dress up as the navy. You'll be playing the role of Commodore St Stephen."

"What's the point?" he demanded. "It's a ridiculous exercise. What does it matter how you get to Port Elizabeth?"

"I too would like to know the answer to the commodore's question," Lysander asked, his sapphire eyes sparkling at me across the table. "You're going to be captured anyway. Does the *how* matter?"

"It matters," I growled. "It matters because it matters to me that I walk in there with the hostages I'm delivering and a ship that Val can get out on. It matters to me that I'm not snatched before I even set foot on the island. They're banking on being able to act in bad faith. And too bad for them, I expect that. Maybe they're even hoping you two don't make it back." The commodore looked stricken at the idea, but Lysander's disgusted sneer told me I'd struck close to the mark. "So I think it's in all of our best interests to get as close to their front door under our own power as possible."

"During this...uniform heist," the commodore asked, with obvious distaste. "Nobody will get hurt?"

"No one that doesn't do anything stupid."

"So just you then," he remarked dryly.

"You're goddamn lucky you're essential to this voyage," I told him as I drained my goblet. "Okay. Here's what we do. We catch one of these outer patrols alone. Steal their clothes. Pass the door check by pretending to be a mixed ship of naval crew and survivors of a pirate attack. Should be easy enough with a bonafide commodore. We land in Port Elizabeth, make the hostage exchange and get out. Old man Grimstead can cry into his pillow that he has to honour his word. Everyone got it?"

Everyone at the table nodded, except the commodore who looked like he'd swallowed a live frog and Dauntless who was still chortling.

"Good. Meeting over. Now. Everyone, out."

"Oh, I'm not going anywhere," Lysander said.

13

———————

"Yes, yes you are," I told him firmly. "Don't worry, I haven't forgotten our *arrangement*. It's just that my to-do list has a few more things on it before I get to you. Like getting my stitches checked and bringing Dauntless up to speed."

Lysander's jewel-like eyes flicked to Dauntless who had finished his meal and was now casually sharpening a pocket knife. When he wasn't spending half his time as a parrot and got to pick his own wardrobe, he was immaculately styled. But even now in the ragtag attire we mustered up for his broad frame, he managed to look handsome and dangerous. There wasn't a scar or abrasion that didn't somehow increase his attractiveness and he absolutely knew it.

Thank god the man had such big shoulders. He needed them to carry that massive ego.

Lysander's eyes slid back to mine. "You're mistaken about what I want."

"I highly doubt that." I stood up, and pushed open the

door to my cabin, sweeping my arm to indicate everyone should clear out. "Someone send in Doc."

Everyone trooped out of my cabin except Dauntless. I poured us both another drink.

"You're not hiding out in my cabin forever, Edward," I told him. "It's beneath you."

"I wasn't planning to." He scowled, those chiseled features bunching up petulantly. "You said you wanted to talk. We can talk while Doc checks your back. I could've done it for you, you know. I've patched you up enough times."

"Then we wouldn't be doing much talking. You'd get distracted." I shrugged. "Either by pitching a fit about how reckless I am or getting distracted by my boobs."

"I can be a professional," he said, immediately undermining his own words by putting his boots on the table and picking something out of his teeth with a knife.

"A professional scoundrel." I stuck my tongue out at him. The frown gave way to a smile, and he huffed, something like a tired laugh.

The cabin door opened and Doc came in. I shucked off my shirt and turned my chair backwards so they could see my back easily. Dauntless made a disappointed noise, since he wouldn't be able to see the girls.

I snorted. Thanks be to Davy Jones and his infinite rest that Doc was here to do the honours of checking my wounds. The last thing I needed was complicated sex with Dauntless, which had almost happened in the early hours of that morning. We were only saved by coitus interruptus parrotus. But him perving on me was an amusing contrast to the commodore.

"Have you taken it easy on your stitches today?" Doc

asked, with the resigned air of someone who knew I was about as likely to say yes as I was to take vows as a nun.

"Well. I didn't get into any fights, have any sex or lift anything too heavy," I said.

"Not for lack of trying," Dauntless said. His eyes were suddenly heavy lidded as he regarded me. I wanted to throw something at him, but Doc would get upset.

"That's better than I usually get from you, captain." Doc ignored Dauntless entirely. "Hmm. No blood on the bandages. That's a good sign." They unwound the bandages with practiced steadiness. There was an audible gasp as the bandages fell away.

"Doc?" I tried to twist around to see my own back. "Doc, what's wrong?"

Doc swore in another language, and put their cold fingers on my back. It didn't hurt but there was an uncomfortable pulling sensation. I yelped.

Dauntless leapt to his feet and in two large strides closed the ground between us. His hand snapped out to grab Doc's wrist, but they pulled it away with the quickness of a rattlesnake.

"If you hurt her—" Dauntless's voice died in his throat. "Should it look like that?"

"No," Doc said emphatically. "And if you try to touch me again I'll sew your balls to your face."

"Okay, very funny, very funny. Now someone tell me what's going on before I have you both thrown overboard." I'd never actually throw Doc overboard. A doctor on a ship was worth almost more than everyone else combined.

"Nothing," Dauntless said. "There's nothing."

"Dauntless, shut the fuck up—"

"Your wounds have gone, captain," Doc spoke over me. "You were an absolute mess last night when I stitched you up. The commodore was doubtful you'd escape an infection especially since the area of the injury is highly mobile. But in less than twenty four hours, your wound has closed completely leaving only a scar ridge. I've never seen anything like this in my entire life."

"But hurt today, when I moved..." I trailed off uncertainly.

Now that I thought about it, it didn't hurt as much as it should have. I hadn't taken anything for pain since I'd woken up and I'd been as sober as a judge all day, apart from a few drinks with dinner. I remember how much my back had hurt last night. It should have hurt a fuck of a lot more today than it did.

"More than likely that was the stitches pulling." Doc deftly snipped the thread that the commodore had so painstakingly woven into my flesh the previous night. Within minutes, they had removed them all. "You can put your shirt on. I'm not needed anymore. If you happen to find out who did this or how, send them Elspeth's way. She needs all the help she can get." Seeing the stormy look on my face, they added, "that is, if you still want her alive." With a nod, they gathered up their things.

As they turned to leave my cabin, a thought struck me. "You don't seem perplexed by seeing Captain Dauntless."

"I heard he was in the battle last night. I presumed he either survived or he's a ghost now, and he's making far too much noise to be a ghost." They looked Dauntless up and down. "There doesn't seem much point in questioning things that are in front of my eyes. My life would be easier if people spent less time gawping and more time reacting." With a shrug, they left my cabin to return to their primary patient.

Doc was ever the pragmatist.

Dauntless had returned to his seat as I pulled my shirt back on, and settled comfortably back in my chair.

"Wizard-boy?" he asked.

"What?"

"Your back. Reckon wizard boy did it?"

I shook my head. "He'd gloat if it was him."

"Who else on this ship is hiding magical powers?" He threw his hands in the air. "I'm sick of this hocus pocus bullshit, Magpie."

"Well, for once it came in on our side which is a welcome change."

"We have no idea what strings are attached. You know as well as I do there's nothing free in the world that you don't take for your own damn self." He glowered at nothing in particular and drummed his fingers on the table. "There's a price. You just don't know what it is yet."

I shifted uncomfortably. "What exactly do you want me to do about it? Slice my back open again?"

"Of course not." He gritted his teeth, his magnificent jawline hardening. He looked away, the warm candlelight dancing on his cool light brown skin, his usually meticulous beard now slightly unkempt by the trials of the last few days. Dauntless always ran a tight ship when he had his own way. He planned more than I did. He was an opportunist and a risk taker, but he calculated his odds more carefully than I did. These odds we were facing? Terrible. These plans we had? Haphazard at best.

"This is a shitshow, Magpie." His eyes glittered. "We're sailing into a situation that's set up to fuck us in more ways than Val's Pleasure Emporium. It'll be a small miracle if we make it in, and I don't know how you imagine on getting out."

"Got any bright ideas to improve our odds of not being absolutely minced?" I asked.

"Dammit Maggie." He swung his legs off the table and grabbed my forearms. His chair landed with a heavy thump. "These people are trying to *kill* you. They're not fucking around."

"They are, actually," I spat back, trying to shake off his grip but failing. "Seems like they have plenty of ways to kill me real fast but they're going the long way around. I've been thinking and it seems like whatever they want me for, before they kill me, they need me in Port Elizabeth first."

"That's fine then. We'll just sail in, let them do what that is, and hope they let you walk out afterwards?"

"What is wrong with you?" I jumped to my feet, finally breaking his grip. He stood too and we were practically toe to toe, each of us vibrating with anger. "Did your brain stay as a parrot brain? No, I walk in and then you and Val and everyone else figure out how to get me the fuck out. I thought that was obvious. Then we blow Port Elizabeth to Davy Jones' locker."

"What if we can't get you out?"

This seemed to be the question that had been burning in Dauntless. There was real fear in it, something I had rarely heard from him. His face hardened when he saw I'd heard it, and he swiped glasses and tankards off the table. Dull thuds and the tinkle of glassware filled the room.

"What the fuck am I supposed to do if we can't get you out?" he roared, anger eclipsing every other emotion.

I grabbed him by the front of the shirt. "Then you blow Port Elizabeth to Davy Jones' locker anyway because we both know that's where I'm gonna end up one day."

He looked lost, for a moment. The great Captain Dauntless without a heading. That's all right. I'd give him something to do.

I pressed my mouth hard against his.

14

His mouth tasted of rum and sweat for the brief seconds that he kissed me back, before pushing me away.

"You're distracting me," he growled, keeping me at arm's length with one hand and wiping his lips with the other. *Ouch, that's unnecessary.* "You think kissing me is going to distract me from the fact you just asked me to blow you to Davy Jones' locker if everything turns to shit?"

"I didn't ask." I sank back into my seat, crossing my arms and huffing. "I ordered."

Dauntless made a wordless noise in his throat, somewhere between a gurgle and a growl.

"And I didn't order you to destroy me, I ordered you to destroy Port Elizabeth. It just so happens I might be in it at the time." I hiked an eyebrow. "Any real pirate would be leaping at the chance."

"Woman, don't insult me by pretending—"

There was a hammering on the door. "Captain Flint, if

you don't want to see this boat grind to a halt in the ocean, I suggest you keep our appointment."

Dauntless's dark eyes glittered for a moment at me, then he crossed the cabin in a few strides of his long legs and wrenched open the door.

"You can't—" I swiped a book off one of the shelves and threw it at him. It bounced off his back as Dauntless yanked the irritating sorcerer inside.

"I've had enough of her bullshit," my ex-lover told the blond aristocrat. "You can have some." He disappeared out onto the deck, slamming the cabin door behind him.

The silence following was almost louder than the slamming door.

"Did I interrupt a lovers' tiff?" Lysander asked.

"No, he's just being uncharacteristically sentimental. Have a seat—or do you want me to stand? How do you want to do this?" He was only there to jump my bones. Even though I hadn't gotten laid in ages, I couldn't muster any excitement at the prospect.

"I told you, I'm not here for that." He threw himself in the seat opposite me, long lanky legs hanging over the side, cobalt blue eyes regarding me. "I don't actually fuck unwilling partners. Yesterday... well, I said things I didn't mean while I was angry and horny. I'm sure you know the feeling."

"Too well." I grabbed a tankard that Dauntless had missed and went to fill it.

"So I'm going to take my time seducing you." I made a noise of disbelief. Lysander shot me a venomous look that would've put any of Judith's snakes to shame. "Oh, I know I'm not any of the walking broadsides of a ship you like to ogle but I've got my own charms."

"Yeah? When are you planning to start employing them?"

I sat back down with my fresh drink. I set the tankard down and leaned forward, a smile playing on my lips.

Lysander's smile answered mine, supercilious with an edge of playfulness. He produced a short nub of chalk from somewhere on his person and pushed aside the map, exposing the mottled wooden tabletop that divided us. "I'm going to show you a magic trick." I opened my mouth to protest and he held up a finger to stop me. "A small one. You can stop it anytime by wiping your sleeve across it."

After a moment, I nodded. He'd be mad to try anything. If something happened to me, he'd be dead before he reached Port Elizabeth.

"I knew you were a daredevil."

He had me there.

He placed the white chalk against the pitted dark wood of the table and drew first one circle, then a second one, about a foot apart, the circles the size of a decent sized plate, the kind you'd get at an okay tavern, and he filled them with symbols I didn't recognise.

I watched, fascinated, as he filled the first circle and started on the second one. It was only then I realised he'd been whispering to himself, a soft susurration that now seemed to come from all around. I shifted in my chair as the fine hairs on my neck, then on my arms and legs, stood up. The air felt heavy, as though it were laden with lightning before a storm.

Just as I was about to say enough is enough, he lifted the chalk from the table and all the whispering ceased. The air deflated, if air could even do that, and he looked at me with a smile that held just an edge of teeth.

"Before you ask what that was, the answer is magic."

"I know *that*." I had absolutely been about to ask what the fuck that had been.

"Mmm." He held one of his hands palm up over one of the circles and nodded at me. "If you would, stroke my palm."

"Is this some kind of wizard kink?"

"Somebody's wizard kink, I am certain, but it's a subject I avoid discussing with my sorcerer associates. I think their exotic tastes would shock even my accommodating sensibilities." He nodded down at his palm. "Go on."

I reached out with a finger and slowly, gently, began to trace swirls across his palms, running my index finger up and down his soft hand, uncalloused by hard work.

"Is something supposed to happen?" I asked after a few seconds.

Instead of replying, he reached across the table and took my other hand, pulling it over the other circle. As he did so, tingles erupted across my hand, and I felt a featherlight touch of a calloused finger running up my palm -

I jerked back in shock.

"Go on," he said. "It's completely harmless."

"Neptune's balls, that's weird," I breathed. I stuck my hand back over the circle. My breath practically stopped as I traced his hand and felt the sensation mirrored on my own hand.

After a minute or so, Lysander took his free hand, delicately placed a finger between his lips and before I realised what he was doing, dragged a wet line down my palm. The unexpected sensation shot down both my hands and spread up my arms in goosebumps. I could see a shiver run up his arm too.

He leaned back, withdrawing his arms and crossing them across his body. "Can you imagine what fun we could have with that party trick that's not tickling each others' palms?" His eyes gleamed.

"Aye," I said, trying for nonchalant but coming out breathless instead. "We could definitely get in a few orgasms before I remember your family's trying to kill me."

"To be honest with you, they don't like me much either." He smirked, but it lacked heart. "Whatever reason my father has for rescuing me, it isn't merely paternal love, I am certain."

"I want you to promise to help me get out of there in one piece."

"I'm not in the business of daring rescues."

"I'm not asking you to fire a crossbow and sever the rope at my hanging, you dolt. I'm asking you to use your amazing ability to run your mouth and hocus pocus to negotiate me out of some back door before I have to go to a hanging or a ritual sacrifice or whatever it is that's coming my way." His pale brows furrowed. "It'll almost certainly piss your dad off."

He tilted his head, considering.

"You know what? It's no skin off my nose." He shrugged. "If I'm free of your ship, I'll see what I can do about helping you get free."

"Great. Now your odds of getting in my pants are looking better, wizard boy."

15

Bright and early the next morning, I told the crew we were holding up a navy ship to steal their clothes.

"Aye, but what for, captain?" One of Val's crew asked after a stunned silence. "Their clothes ain't much to look at."

"Not to naysay yer orders, captain," Sharky added, dipping his head respectfully, "but what's the value in navy men's duds? If you say they're valuable, I'll go steal every pair of tight white britches on the seas. It just tickles my curiosity, is all."

I flashed a wide grin, no doubt further convincing my crew that I had, finally, gone completely mad. "Port Elizabeth is more closely guarded than a virgin noble's bedchamber. If Haddrick and Mercer can nab us without paying up their half of the bargain, so much the better for them, aye?" I spread my arms. "But they say to never trick a trickster for a good reason. We're going to waltz in the front door as a navy crew. No one will have any reason to doubt us—not with the commodore to vouch for us."

For several seconds you could've heard a pin drop on deck

as the crew absorbed this plan. I leaned easily against the railing of the top deck, as if my heart weren't hammering in my chest, half expecting a second mutiny in as many weeks.

Raucous laughter rang out from the deck below and I grinned, swallowing my relief down. Dauntless the parrot swooped past, cawing, and clipping me on the back of the head with a wing. I grinned at him. He was the only one who'd believed in my plan last night. Bit awkward when only your ex is backing you, but then, he'd been the only one in that room who'd seen how many of my crazy plans had come together.

As the commodore predicted, we intercepted a lone navy patrol vessel several hours later. The boarding crew were bristling with arms, and had been briefed by both myself and the commodore. The latter had told them what to expect on a naval ship, and I had told them what I wanted. Our mast was flying Haddrick and Mercer colours, as well as a flag requesting urgent aid.

It was clear when the navy vessel saw us and began to change heading towards us. Its broadside dotted with cannons yawned at us, and I swallowed bile. If the ruse wasn't convincing, all they would have to do was fire those cannons and we'd be on our way to Davy Jones's locker without a chance to defend ourselves.

"They won't fire," the commodore said, sensing my unease. He was kneeling next to me, his voice muffled into the bandana he'd wrapped around his face. He was almost unrecognisable now but he didn't want to take any chances.

I could relate. After all, I hadn't wanted anyone in the Last Doubloon to know that I was running around with the commodore. We were hell on each others' reputation.

"How do you know that?" I kept my spyglass trained on

the ship. I hated how slowly things moved on the ocean sometimes. Dauntless and Val had called me a creature of instant gratification, usually in exasperated tones, but what was the point in delay when I might be dead the next day?

"Protocol," the commodore said simply. "You live by your whims, we live by strict rules. Besides," he added, "even if they do, we have a wizard."

Lysander was set up in a new box fort on the deck, with Judith assisting, drawing complicated chalk drawings.

"Lucky us," I muttered with rancour I didn't really feel. The image of the cannonball volley dropping into the sea just shy of hitting my ship had been burned into my memory. One of the few cherished memories from the battle at the Last Doubloon.

"Before I go below, can I register my absolute opposition and disgust at this plan once more?" The commodore turned toward me.

"Registered." I pretended to write it down, sign it, and put the invisible paper in my pocket. "Is there anything else?"

"Magpie Flint, stop being a fool and look at me." The force in his words sent a shiver up my spine—adrenaline did strange things to me—and my eyes were drawn to his like a magnet. They burned like coal. Oh, the bastard looked like a buccaneer through and through now.

"What?" I hissed. "Do you want a goodbye kiss?"

Please say yes. The thought popped unbidden into my head.

"Focus, Flint, I'm being deadly serious." He pulled the bandana off, angling his back towards the coming ship, and his expression was as serious as a hanging. "You're not to hurt anyone, remember?"

"I'm not going to hurt anyone who doesn't do anything stupid."

"Flint. I gave up my people to you. Their lives are on my head."

"Commodore, this is a robbery. I intend to leave with the goods, and zero blood spilled, and not just because that'll ruin the merchandise. But," I put my finger over his lips as he tried to start talking again. "If one of your ensigns or lieutenants or cosigns goes off half cocked, I'm going to handle it. There's a lot of male ego on one boat. It's a bit of a powder keg."

The commodore's jaw hardened to the point I was surprised I couldn't hear his teeth cracking.

"I won't start the fight but I'll finish it, if it comes to it." I looked at the unhappy, desperately handsome navy man in front of me. "Cheer up, commodore. I still want to seduce you before we get to Port Elizabeth, so I'm going to be on my best behaviour over there. Now go hide below before you're spotted and someone tries to do something stupid and heroic."

I couldn't tell if that last bit had reassured him, scared him or turned him on. I was crossing my fingers for the last one, but if I was honest, I knew I was just making myself laugh ahead of danger. As the commodore disappeared safely into the hold, I stood up and let out a sharp whistle.

The boarding party moved into position, still looking as casual as possible so the navy spotters didn't see more than a ship at work. I went up to Lysander's box fort of sorcery and peered over. He sat cross legged, palms up, a gesture that reminded me of our strange encounter last night and sent a tingle up my arm. His eyes were shut and he was mouthing words soundlessly.

"Remember." I kicked one of his crates lightly. "If you betray us, I will strangle you with your own entrails before I die."

"You're all stick and no carrot, Flint," Lysander murmured, without opening his eyes. "I am a very reward motivated man, you should keep that in mind."

"Your reward is your entrails staying where they should be." I glanced up. "All right. It's show time."

"Only you would characterise the beginning of hostilities in the same manner as other people start a theatre performance."

"It's all a show, wizard boy, and you know it."

A genuine smile curled on his face, lighting up the handsome lines of his jaw and cheekbones in a way I hadn't seen them before. It gave me a second's pause, but then I shook my head to clear it. Time to get my head in the game.

The navy ship was pulling up alongside us. I made my way over to the middle of my boarding party. I had two flintlocks securely tucked into my belt, and a long dagger strapped to my back.

"Peggy!" I called. She triggered her reassembled ballista. A second later, something whizzed overhead, landing on the navy ship. "Eyes!"

Our entire crew averted their eyes. Though we couldn't see, we heard the bangs and pops as well as the surprised reactions from the crew on the other ship.

"What exactly is that?" Sharky asked from a little way down the line.

"It's harmless, just a little lightshow. We traded for it with someone who got it from the East." I sprang to my feet, and gave the signal. With the navy crew distracted and blinded by the pyrotechnics, we crossed the gap between the ships with ease. In what felt like seconds, we were standing on a navy ship, pointing our flintlocks at two dozen startled redcoats and their captain.

"Ahoy, mateys," I said with a grin. "I'm Captain Magpie Flint, and this here is a robbery. Put your hands in the air and give us all your clothes."

16

"I beg your pardon. Give you all our *what*?" A man with a coat far fancier and a wig far stupider than the others demanded in an accent so nasal I was surprised to see his mouth moving rather than his nostrils.

"Your *clothes*," I repeated with exaggerated slowness. "I want your uniforms, sailor. I normally entertain people with my witty repartee before getting them out of their duds but time is pressing, and none of you are my type. So please, if you would all just climb out of your uniforms and hand them over, we'll be on our merry way. You'll have nary a scratch on your fine persons and this will be an excellent story to tell at whatever hole you like you drink at. Oh—" I gestured up at the mast. "We'll be taking your colours too."

"This ship," the captain said, drawing himself to his full height, "is—"

"Sorry, who the fuck are you?" I pointed my gun directly at him.

"I *beg* your *pardon*?" His eyebrows nearly touched his wig.

"Is that the only thing you can say? I see how you got to

be captain, all that begging," I replied, aiming my pistol carefully. "Anyway, I like to know who I'm threatening."

The captain looked me up and down, appraising me. I must have been quite a sight. I'd dressed to impress after all. My cleanest black leather boots, harem pants, silk scarves around my waist and a weapon rack around my waist that really accentuated the second most important rack (in this situation anyway). Oh, and jewelry. I was wearing a lot of gold, because I knew there were three languages the British Empire spoke: violence, wealth and English. I was a riot of colour, bristling with gold and weapons. With my feet apart, guns in hand, I announced in every language they knew that I meant business.

I was everything they could expect from the Caribbean's most wanted. Except, I suppose, my rather strange demand for their clothes.

"You've taken quite a gamble coming on board here," the captain said at last. "Even though you've caught us unawares, you still have to make a retreat. Even if you disable the cannons, you must out sail us before we fix them and catch you."

"That won't be a problem, but it's sweet of you to care." I blew him a kiss.

He ignored it.

Everyone else on board stayed perfectly still as they watched the negotiations proceed. Good to know there were no heroes in the navy.

"I'm going to assume you're not here on a suicide mission just for some clothes. There must be something else you want."

"The colours," I reminded him. "Oh, and the wigs. No navy disguise is complete without those wigs."

He mulled it over. His men waited like sheep for a decision. A mulish look crossed his face and I knew his decision before they did.

I lined him up in my sights.

"Men!" he barked.

I fired.

There was the whizz of the shot as it flew and the captain's wig went flying. Seconds later, red flowed from his bald scalp.

Damn, I'd nicked him.

"It's just a scratch," I shouted as the navy crew stirred and cried out restlessly. "Head wounds bleed like a son of a bitch. He'll be fine. Who's the ship's surgeon here? You?"

An older sailor, all the way in his thirties, waved a hand. "Sebastian, take the doctor up there to look at him. Which of you sheep is next in line, and are you going to be less of a moron?"

"That'd be me." The man that stepped forward sounded far less nasally, thank god. He was shorter, leaner and looked like he actually worked. The whimpering and cursing from the man with the scratch made me wonder if he was just appointed because he inherited the right title. They did insane things like that in the navy, picking people for jobs based on their name rather than their ability to do the work. Amazing they got anything done.

The new man I was addressing approached slowly, hands in the air, stopping a respectful distance from me.

"Lieutenant Thomas Hattsford of His Majesty's Ship *Perseverance*." He took his eyes off me briefly to glance at the surgeon. "Morton, will the captain recover?"

"Just a scratch," the surgeon called back. "The wench is

87

right. Scalp wounds bleed like nobody's business. He probably won't even have a scar."

"I want her in chains!" the captain whimpered.

"He's—he's passed out from—the blood loss." Morton
added after a second. We all knew that was a lie. The bilgerat
either couldn't handle the sight of blood or was just
pretending to faint so that someone else would handle this.
"He can't lead the ship right now."

I raised an eyebrow at the lieutenant.

"As the captain is currently incapacitated," he said, "and I
am acting captain, we will not be throwing you in chains."

"You're a smart lad. I hope you get promoted soon," I told
him cheerfully. "Now, give your guns and wigs to my crew,
hop out of your clothes, fetch the colours, and we'll be on our
way."

The seamen all looked at their lieutenant in confusion
and panic.

"Captain Flint, you can't actually be serious—"

"I am deadly serious," I snapped. "We'll bring you other
clothes that you can wear until you get back to port. They're
far more comfortable and look a hell of a lot better too. Trust
me, you're getting the better end of the deal here." I had a
thought. "And that's outer clothes only. For the love of the sea,
keep your undergarments on, we don't want those."

"Thanks for clarifying, Captain Flint." The lieutenant
shucked his coat over his shoulder with a venomous look. "I
wasn't sure how far your mad demands went."

"All the personal pistols can stay in their holsters, thank
you very kindly." I barely repressed a shudder.

"Aye but what about the personal cannons?" A seaman
called from the far end of the deck.

"Lad, if you had a cannon tucked away there, surely you'd

have fired it and saved you all from this indignity," I called back, while I menaced one particularly slow undresser with my flintlock.

"You come see my cannon and you'll forget about all of this I promise you."

"I have all the cannons I need, sailor. I don't want to get in your trousers. I just need them off you."

This was yet again an entry on the list of things I didn't expect to be doing in my glamorous life as a dashing pirate captain, but needs must when Magnus Grimstead shits all over your life. My crew were collecting up the (actual) guns, clothes, wigs and the like, while others made sure no one was up to any funny business. Funny-dangerous, that is. I hoped the navy lads would be able to laugh about it. I made a mental note to leave them a barrel of something to drink.

I was distracted from the paltry excuse for witty repartee by an exchange that was escalating in tension. I elbowed my way through partially clothed navy men.

"Captain says you gotta take your clothes off, or we shoot you." Sharky pointed a gun at a sailor of medium build with fine, clean shaven features, who had his arms crossed tightly and had his face set in hard defiance.

"Then you're going to have to shoot me. I'm not taking my clothes off."

"Whoa, whoa, sailor, is this really worth losing your life over?" I smiled disarmingly.

"Yes. I would rather die." His eyes met mine. I was taken aback to see the fierceness in them was fuelled by fear, not anger. I stared back for a few moments, caught under the weight of the feeling. I nodded slowly, once.

"You know what, there's more than enough translucent flesh on display, we don't need to add more. It must be true about England never seeing any sun if you all look like bloody porcelain." I glanced at the young man, who seemed surprised to not currently be sporting a bullet hole. "You. Go below and get any spare uniforms and wigs from down there. Don't try anything funny. I've heard what passes for a sense of humour around here and it stinks worse than low tide after the dead wash up."

Shoulders relaxing, the sailor nodded and without a fuss, descended below deck.

"Why'd you go easy on him?" Sharky complained, frustrated.

I didn't blame him, he was young, a lot of things he hadn't seen yet. "Folk who'd rather be shot than take their clothes off usually have good reason. Only lads are allowed in the navy but say someone has a powerful urge to sail, you see?" I waited for the doubloon to drop. "Or perhaps he's one of those lads whose exterior came out all mixed up."

"Aye, captain, I see yer point. Me cousin was a lad like that. Folks get all sort of stirred up for no reason on that account."

"I don't think he'll cause trouble, but wait here for him and be prepared," I told my sailor, before turning to check on the rest of proceedings.

The deck was covered by a partially naked, partially underclothed crew of His Majesty's Royal Navy, Some of them were indeed as pale as I had joked, obviously on their first trip out of the homeland, while others bore the tan of having lived in the Caribbean for some time already. Most were in their underwear, what the Brits called 'pants' though some chose to defy that edict—or had not bothered to put any on—and everything was on display, garnering friendly ribaldry from my crew and some offers that sailed right past flirtatious and into bawdy. Reactions ranged between outraged and tempted.

Gathering up the clothes, transferring them over to our ship, and giving them a batch of our spare clothes in return was quick work. Lieutenant Thomas Hattsford toed the bundle suspiciously, picking up a faded shirt that had once been a bright red, with a magnificently loose fit. He gave me a look that told me he'd rather wring my neck with the shirt than wear it.

"I happen to think those are very comfortable," I told him. "Red *is* your colour, isn't it? Smart choice. Doesn't show blood. Regardless, gentlemen, I thank you." I moved backwards to the railing of the ship as we prepared to return to *The Queen's Liberty*, our heist successfully completed. I hopped up on the railing and holstered my gun as I grabbed a rope. "My apologies for any indignities, if you have any complaints, you can direct them straight to Magnus—"

I didn't hear the shot, I just felt the burning pain below my left shoulder as it spun me off balance.

I hovered there, poised on the edge of the ship's railing on one foot, extended too far over the water for what felt like an eternity. The hand that had been holding the rope dropped slack, all the strength drained from it.

Then I plummeted into the ocean, darkness swallowing me up.

17

Complete darkness.

An all consuming cold.

The unfathomable

D

E

E

P

S

18

"*H nnngh!*" I gasped, bright sunlight in my eyes as my head broke above water. A strong body held me, keeping me above the waves even as my deadweight wanted to sink. There had been an argument. Someone was there that I didn't know—and someone I did know—in the deeps —deeps no one could survive... I chased these fragments of thoughts that slid from me like the last elusive wisps of a dream.

A familiar voice brought me back to reality. "There you are, captain. Can you breathe?" It was Sebastian. He was the one holding me, his long legs elegantly and nearly effortlessly paddling to keep us afloat.

"Yes," I said, but it sounded more like *hnnngh* again. I vomited seawater back into the sea. "I got shot."

"You're not bleeding," Sebastian said after a second. "Maybe it missed you."

Missed me? That information was so jarring it sent my world spinning. I nearly flopped out of Sebastian's arms, forcing him to heave me up above the waterline again.

It didn't *miss me*. I was as certain that I'd been shot as I was that my name was Magdalene Flint. But I didn't have the energy to argue as Sebastian swam us over to a sling lowered by *The Queen's Liberty*.

It hadn't even finished hauling us up before Lysander used his magic to summon up some impressive speeds and start putting distance between us and the navy ship. To their credit, they didn't even try a cannon volley.

"What happened?" I croaked, leaning into the warm line of Sebastian's body. He was the most warm and uncomplicated thing in the world right now.

"The lieutenant," Sebastian said, tension racing through his body for a moment. "He shot at you."

"Damn, and there I was thinking he was smart." I coughed, the kind of cough that racks your whole body, and spat bloody saliva. Sebastian held on tight so I didn't fall out of the sling. We finally reached the deck of the ship and he helped me over the railing. Mercifully, I was able to stand upright—as long as I could lean on him.

Doc was already there, a wad of bandages in hand. "Lie her down, lie her down. It's a miracle she's alive! We need to staunch the bleeding."

"The shot missed," Sebastian said. "It must have just thrown her off balance."

Doc stared at him, then looked at me. I looked down too, and took in the fact that my white shirt and gold waistcoat were not marred by blood.

"But I saw..." Doc frowned, and pressed their hand against my upper left chest.

Memories of the wound I thought I had received made it ache, and I winced. This was enough for Doc to pull open the waistcoat and unlace the neck of the shirt and deftly prod my intact flesh.

Only Doc gets away with manhandling me like that without dinner.

"My mistake." They leaned back, perplexed and a little unhappy. They didn't leave, merely stood there, bandages still in hand, as if waiting for a delayed reaction gunshot to spontaneously erupt. Hell, that wouldn't even be the strangest thing that happened in the last three days.

Smith came over next. "Captain, with ye being uninjured, I'm well pleased to report the mission was a success, such as this farce of a mission could be called that. We have the goods, no injuries or fatalities on our side, and only one fatality on the other side."

"Fatality? Who died?"

"The son of a landlubber who shot at ye, cap'n," Smith said, with satisfaction. "Tweren't me that shot him and I swear on me mother's grave if I knew who did I would tell ye, but ye were shot at and fair all of us was convinced ye were hit and a goner. Sebastian here took off at a sprint and dove into the water after ye, but he'd barely taken five steps when a shot rang out from this ship and nailed the bastard. They couldn't fire back on us because we'd taken all their guns—'cept that one that the bastard had hidden somehow—so there was a bit of fisticuffs until their captain on the top deck came to and told them all to let us go."

I *knew* that bilgerat captain had been faking.

"Well, that went as well as could be hoped, really." I pulled away from Sebastian and stood on my own two feet. Excellent. Nary a wobble. I wish I didn't look like a drowned rat but you can't have everything.

"Thanks for saving my life, Sebastian," I told him.

He smiled at me, his eyes burning into mine, but there were deep lines of tiredness around his mouth I hadn't seen before. "I will never let anything happen to you, captain." He leaned his forehead against mine, his voice a fierce whisper. "I will protect you; you can rely on that."

I blinked, surprised, touched and suspicious. The commodore's warnings about him from the previous day came back to me. What did I really know about Sebastian? Could I trust his earnest desire to protect me? Looking into his eyes, I wanted to...

"It makes a nice change from all the people wanting to kill me." It was meant to be flippant, but it came out breathy. I don't *do* breathy.

I took a large step back and shook my head. Smith had thankfully removed himself from the situation and our exchange had been relatively private, for all that it was on the deck of a busy ship.

"Judith!" I called. The small witch appeared moments later. "Get some people, and start sorting all these clothes by size and whatnot. Figure out who fits what. And find the commodore. We're going to get a crash course in being part of the British Navy."

19

That night I dreamt of the deeps again. I was on my back, sinking, sinking down, the light of the surface stretching away before disappearing altogether. There was only darkness and cold, now and a heaviness that dragged me further below. I knew I didn't need to struggle. The ocean cradled me. My limbs relaxed, my spine softened and my head tilted back.

Time to sleep on the bottom of the ocean.

An iridescent shape caught my eye before my eyelids fluttered shut, coming at me impossibly fast. I tried to thrash but my limbs were no longer responding to my commands.

As the shape grew closer, I recognised it. Sebastian. *What was he doing here?*

Maybe he lived here. The thought was irrational, but he looked so natural in the water.

He swam up to me, and caught me in his arms, pressing his hand against my chest. Warmth and life shot through my limbs. He kissed me and his breath filled my lungs. The burning need to breathe abated.

None of this made sense. I'm making out with Sebastian halfway to the bottom of the ocean. For a moment he is my sun, my heartbeat and my oxygen.

"How is this possible?" I try to say, but the words are lost as seawater presses in at the slightest opening of my mouth.

"It's a dream," Sebastian whispers.

A dream. I cling to him as he begins to swim towards the surface.

A voice, so enormous it makes my teeth rattle and my bones ache, pulses out a single word that I felt rather than heard.

No.

A current that sprung up out of nowhere ripped me away from Sebastian. I hung suspended in the water.

Sebastian, lit by his own strange light, twisted around, and tried to move towards me, before another current knocked him away.

Did you think you could do this quickly and I wouldn't notice? The voice moaned like ship hulls thrashing at their moorings during a storm.

"She needs to live!' Sebastian shouted to the darkness. "I have a right to use my power. It is mine."

It belongs to the sea and the sea will have its due. You cannot cheat it, boy. SHE cannot cheat it.

Despite the obvious direness of the situation, I desperately wanted to make a quip about how lying, stealing and cheating were basically all I aspired to in life. It was for the best that I couldn't talk.

As if sensing my ever-present perverse desire to ruin a good thing, Sebastian shot me a warning look. "I'll settle it. Just let her go."

The stillness is deafening. Almost as deafening as the voice when it speaks again.

You are lucky you are my favourite, Sebastian. Few else would get away with this. I tasted her blood when she hit the water. But know this, if she cheats me again, the debt will be on her and it will not be so easy for her to settle a debt such as this.

I really hoped this was just a dream, because I didn't need any more problems, and whoever this creature—thing—was, it sounded like a big problem.

Whatever dream magic had been holding me up was suddenly gone. I sank like a stone.

Sebastian scooped me up in his arms in a flash, pressing me against him as he swam upwards at an impossible speed.

I had so many questions I wanted to ask him, but I couldn't open my mouth or my eyes as we rushed through the ocean.

"You don't need to worry about that, captain," he said, somehow speaking despite the rushing seawater. "It's just a dream. A strange dream. If you remember anything, remember I care for you. I'll keep you safe. I'll protect you. You're too important to die."

Then the world exploded in light.

20

———

I woke up with my heart pounding, images from the nightmare playing over and over in my head. The certainty of death as I sank into the abyss. The primal terror at the voice as old as the ocean. Every second of it felt real. Like a memory, not a dream.

I sat up and rolled my left shoulder, only to meet no stiffness or resistance. I wasn't shot, I reminded myself. And if I was, then there's nothing left to show it, so I'd never know unless—

"*Aha!*" I shouted, forgetting there might be other people sleeping in my cabin. Tough luck to them, it was my cabin, and they were there on my sufferance. "I'm not just a stupid pirate."

"Opinions differ," a male voice argued. I couldn't tell who it was, because his voice was muffled by a pillow.

I lit a lantern and found where I had hastily hung up my wet clothes from the afternoon's unplanned dunk in the ocean. Yanking the vest off the line, I smoothed it between my fingers until I found the left shoulder, tilting it towards the glow of the lantern.

There.

A small ragged hole, burned around the edges.

A chill went down my spine.

Throwing it aside, I grabbed the shirt and with shaking hands, I checked the same.

Another hole with burned edges.

"Fuck." The cold that washed over me was as chill as the ocean depths. "It was real."

"What are you babbling about, pirate?"

The voice was Lysander's. He was sitting up in the commodore's bed, blonde hair tousled and his face softened by sleep.

"Lysander, perfect. Just the person I want." I took the lantern and the damning garments over to the table. "Get up, sit down. Make sure you're wearing pants, at least."

"You want me? Well that's definitely worth giving up some sleep for."

I lit some more lanterns while the sleepy sorcerer staggered over to the table wiping his face and pulling on that cerulean shirt that matched his eyes so well. Banging a fresh bottle of rum on the table, I poured us each a glass.

"Where's Dauntless? And the commodore?"

"Dauntless is sailing the ship, and the commodore is fussing over the details for tomorrow's naval hoodwink, so I stole his bed." Lysander shrugged. "I believe in asking for forgiveness not permission."

"Have you ever asked for forgiveness in your life?"

"Come to think of it, no, no I haven't." He shrugged daintily, with a quirk of his lips.

"And Sebastian?"

"No idea. Look, is this just a roll call or did you drag me out of bed for a good reason?"

"You didn't see me get shot this afternoon, right?"

"No, I was doing exactly as I was told, like a good little wizard prisoner." He rolled his eyes. "It missed though, didn't it? I heard Doc examine you."

"That's what we all thought. There's nothing there." I loosened the laces at the neck of my shirt and shrugged it off my left shoulder, giving him an unobstructed view of my shoulder and also the swell of my breast. I couldn't even fault him for glancing at the latter first, his gaze lingering.

"My *shoulder*, Lysander." I tried to shrug the shirt to cover more of the breast, but the motion only caused it to fall further open. Sigh.

He reached out with his pale fingers, smooth and uncalloused, and traced them over the unblemished flesh. The light touch sent arcs of lightning down my flesh and my nipples tightened.

"No bullet hole, no," he said, definitely not looking at my shoulder.

I swatted his hand away and pulled my shirt back up. "But have a look at these." I showed him the garments. His eyes widened as he saw the places the shot passed through. "There's more."

I told him about the dream—or memory—I'd just had, only I left out all the lovey dovey talk from Sebastian. "And when I came out of the water, I felt like something had happened, but I couldn't remember whatever it was."

Lysander shook his head slowly, swirling the rum in his hand. "There's just something about you, isn't there," he said, more to his glass than me.

"What the hell do you mean?" I drained my glass, thumping the heavy glass vessel I had stolen from the Spanish ambassador in a satisfying way on the wooden table.

The rum flamed all the way down, burning away fear, leaving only anger and frustration. "This is your area of expertise."

"Have you ever been to England?" he asked. I shook my head no. "Well, I'm sure you get the same sort of thing over here—lightning storms. Years and years ago, when I was still a lad, my father was doing experiments with lightning storms. He wanted to know why some trees got hit by lightning more than others. A perfectly ordinary tree on a field with plenty of trees just like it. Yet, more often than not, it'd be the same tree hit every storm. People too, he found. No, Flint, he didn't line up people in lightning storms, I see what you're thinking—" He was right; I was thinking that. "Every couple of villages, there was someone that drew the lightning. Once you were hit by lightning, you were more likely to be hit by lightning than anyone else."

"That's real interesting and all," I said, "but what's it got to do with me?"

"Hold your tongue for a few minutes and I'll get to it. My father became fascinated by these people. I never found out what he did with these people—because yes, at this stage, he was rounding them all up for experiments that probably involved standing in a field during a storm, but I was sent off to school and I forgot about it. When I returned a decade later, he was no longer interested in literal lightning. He was interested in lightning as things that happen, things that—" Lysander shrugged again, and gestured.

"Things happen to *you*, Magpie Flint. Wherever you go, things happen. You are a catalyst for events. You are the tree in the field that attracts lightning. If something can happen, it happens to you."

"That isn't the worst description I've had of me, so I won't complain. So this thing— whatever it was," I picked up the shirt with the pistol hole in it, "this is just another thing that's latched onto me?"

"Yes. Not the shooting. That was just you pissing someone else off. But after. Something powerful and magical is protecting you for reasons unknown. It's *incredible*." Lysander's cobalt blue eyes were lit up, his gestures animated. "This must be why my father wants you. And if he doesn't know about it, this might save you.."

"Thanks," I said, somewhat wryly. "I can't wait to go and stand in a storm, waiting to be hit by lightning."

"The problem with being out of the ordinary, Flint, is that people take notice. You've never had a problem with notoriety before."

"Notoriety was egotistical men with cannons," I replied. "Not deranged old men with magical powers."

"You're going up in the world," Lysander said with a smile that I had to admit was somewhat devastating. His face took on a serious expression, one I was unused to, and he pointed at me. "Did you want me to have a look at your chest?"

"Now why in Neptune's name would I want that?"

He gave me a look like I was a petulant child. "To look magically at where you were shot—or where we think you were shot."

"Oh. You'd be able to tell what happened?" I asked.

Lysander uncoiled his lithe legs and stood. "Certainly. Caster usually leaves at least some information behind if you know how to look."

I watched him produce a piece of chalk from one of the pouches on his belt and start drawing a circle and symbols. "And of course this requires you to deface my cabin floor,"

"Naturally. The first part of being a sorcerer is that absolutely no surface is safe." He glanced up at me from where he was crouched on the floor, with a sardonic lift of his lips. "I apologise for disrupting the pristine state of your cabin."

"It's partially your fault." I put my feet up on the table as I watched him work. "I bet your quarters back home would be a state too if your daddy didn't pay some poor maid to pick up after you. Right now I've got a rotating cast of reprobates using my cabin as an inn—which I never agreed to, by the way, you need to go find yourself a hammock somewhere—so of course it's a mess. The only person here who cleans up after themselves is the commodore."

"Mmm, if you're done complaining, come lie down on this circle." Lysander gestured at the presumably magical squiggles he'd just finished drawing.

I approached it with the suspicion I felt it deserved.

"Your chest goes in the circle. It'd be easier if you took your top off."

"I don't like you enough," I told him, as I lay down. Once again I reflected on the wisdom of irritating people just before I put myself at their mercy.

"Not yet," Lysander said, his eyes glittering. He lowered himself over me, straddling my stomach.

I shot my arms out to grab him. "Whoa there, whatcha doing, wizard boy?"

"Magic," Lysander said, exasperated. "Proximity is important. We've both got our clothes on and I'm certain you have at least half a dozen ways to remove me from your person if I did anything you didn't want. Am I right?"

I made a disgruntled noise of agreement.

Lysander rolled his eyes. "See. Now be quiet, I actually have to do some work."

I let my arms drop beside his knees, which were just inside the circle, tightly clenching my ribcage. His weight was hot and comforting, and I exerted more self control than should have been necessary not to rock up against him. My body wasn't picky, apparently, and was just happy to have the warm weight of a man.

I, however, was picky, and had better options than an irritating posh boy sorcerer. I took a deep breath and pretended I was a plank.

He was murmuring now, syllables I couldn't make out. The fine hair on my body stood on end—not from lust, but from a strange tension that sprang up in the circle. A faint humming came from somewhere around us. Lysander reached down and with one hand pulled aside my shirt.

He opened his eyes, which were not just blue but also glowing silver, like they each held the moon on its fullest night. I distantly heard myself shout "Fuck!" in surprise.

His free hand touched the skin of my chest and all at once, his face went whiter than sailcloth, and his jaw went slack. Terror suffused his features.

Without warning, a whirlpool of water opened directly above him and started to pull him in.

21

I instinctively grabbed his legs just below the waist, and curled my legs around the legs of the heavy wooden table in my cabin. Lysander's head and shoulders disappeared into the whirlpool almost immediately but my acrobatics did a passable job of anchoring the rest of him to the ship. Here's hoping he could breathe in there.

"Lysander, what do I do?" I yelled, tightening my grip on his waist. I was losing ground to the whirlpool by centimetres.

His arms flailed but if he said anything, I couldn't hear it over the roar of the miniature maelstrom that had manifested in my cabin.

I racked my brain frantically.

Magic. Obviously, this was magic. From my dreams I knew Sebastian knew something about sea magic but I couldn't very well fetch him.

Ruining the circle? That's what we'd done when interrupting his brother's ritual. I glanced down. Between our shuffling and the spray of sea water from above, the circle was pretty well fucked already.

Lysander slid further from my grip. I roared in frustration and dug my fingers into his belt, hooking my other arm around his torso to pull him back several inches.

One of the pouches on his belt opened slightly and salt fell into my eyes.

"Just my fucking luck..." I blinked furiously.

Something about salt rang a faint bell.

No time to think. I grabbed the pouch and unceremoniously hefted it into the maelstrom.

"Fuck *off*," I screamed.

As suddenly as it had appeared, the whirlpool vanished, and Lysander—who was soaked from the nipples up—fell on top of me, sending us both sprawling in a heap on the cabin floor.

For a few seconds, we just lay there, catching our breath and gathering our mental strength. Lysander might be more used to magical shit than me but I'll bet my ass that he was as surprised as I was.

He lurched upright and vomited seawater on my cabin floor. "Sorry," he gasped, hunched over. "There was no air—"

"Shhhh." I grabbed my two least favourite pillows off my bed and shoved him back onto the floor, lying beside him. I had an incredible abundance of pillows since Val stored half her crap here. "Shut up. You don't need to talk. Lie on your side. Just breathe. No, don't argue." I nearly yanked his arm out of his socket helping him onto his side. "Drownings are my occupational hazard. I know what to do."

With his blond hair slicked to his head, his cheekbones were more prominent than ever and his eyes glittered like the sea beneath the moon. "You saved my life," he rasped.

"Yeah, well, don't undo my good work now." I didn't like

the way he was looking at me. "I can still shoot you if you annoy me."

"Why did you save my life?"

"I didn't know there'd be an interrogation on it," I snapped. "Because you're part of my boat and I didn't know what would happen if you vanished. Because I need you to swap back to your dad. Because it was my fault you were poking around in that magic, and if I'm gonna get you killed, I'd rather do it on purpose."

"No." His gaze bored into mine. An uncomfortable sweat broke out on my neck and my heartbeat sped up. Great. What had someone else figured out about my motives that I wasn't privy to? "You don't rationalize. You act. I die, too bad. You'll fuck my father over and get what you want some other way. You know what I think?"

His breathing had recovered. Mine wasn't doing so good actually.

"I think," he said, propping himself up on one elbow and looking at me with fathomless eyes. "I think you're extremely possessive. And right now, you consider me yours."

I shot my hand up to grab his wrist as his free hand reached towards me.

He smiled wryly, amused.

"I don't own people," I told him. "I'm not in that trade. Never was, never will be. Any slaver that crosses my path is a dead man."

"Not what I meant. My father wants you to be *his*. An item for his collection."

I snorted. "I don't belong to anyone."

"He's a hard man to convince otherwise."

"Well then, as a fellow pirate once said, we'll put it to the test and see who is right and who is dead." I gripped his wrist to the brink of pain. "Where are you going with this?"

"I wish you could be mine instead," he said softly. "But I'm smarter than my father. I'd like to stay alive, so instead I am content to be yours, while it lasts."

"Did you injure your head in that whirlpool?" I drop his hand, turning on my side to look at him. "You've tried to kill me, now you're…"

"You survive because when things change, you adapt. I do the same. I tried to kill you when I had no other options. My options now are vastly better with you around."

We lay silently, regarding each other.

"It was very old ocean magic," Lysander said.

"That's what you got?" I made a face. "I got that from the dreams."

"No, you got dreams from the dreams." He frowned. "I have facts. When I touched the magic that was used to bring you back, it wanted to devour me. It was…" Lysander's eyes looked beyond me, haunted. "I understood everything you said about the dreams. The age. The hunger."

A cold prickle went down my spine. It had nothing to do with being semi-soaked from the maelstrom. "Bring me back?" I demanded.

"You were nearly dead." Lysander's voice was flat. "Massive magic was used to restore you. Not just restore you, but to snatch you from the jaws of a massive predator. And if I had to guess what that predator was, it was the sea."

"How can—how can Sebastian do that?"

"I haven't the faintest idea, but if I were you, I'd consider trading him to my father in your place."

"Hard pass."

He shrugged as best he could while lying on his side.

"Suit yourself. Now. Are we going to use this adrenaline rush for some ill-advised making out or not?"

I have three excuses for why I kissed him: I felt bad about the whole nearly getting him killed thing, adrenaline and the fact I'd been dwelling on how great he looked for the last ten minutes.

His lips touched mine and there was a jolt of that lightning Lysander had prattled on about, the eerie feeling of my fine hairs standing on end.

"Are you doing magic?" I asked against his lips. "Stop it."

"Nope. Not doing a thing," he whispered back, his lips curling into a brief smirk. "That's just me." Now sitting, he pulled me into his lap.

I tugged at his shirt. "This, gone, now."

"That fast?"

"It's sodden. I'm not cuddling up to you while you're drenched. I'm running out of dry clothes." As he peeled the wet shirt away from his body and over his head, I added. "If anyone's going to be drenched, it's me and you'll have to work for that."

Lysander laughed—the first real laugh I heard out of him. The first laugh that wasn't marred by cruelty or ulterior intentions or a sly jab. His face lightened for a moment with the laugh, before the half amused look of calculation settled back in, lit from behind by carnal heat.

Kissing Lysander was a new experience. I'd been with different kinds of men and women over the years, but fundamentally, they'd all been of the sea in some way. My life revolved around the sea and the seafaring community.

Lysander, despite the thin sheen of seawater that covered his face, hair and chest, was not a man of the sea. Not even magically living inside a pirate ship for more than a year had changed that in essence, he was a man who felt and tasted entirely new to me.

I ran my fingers over the fine cheekbones of his face, so razor sharp they rivalled even Dauntless's. His face was so smooth, he must shave daily, and his skin was so pale, I broke from kissing him to marvel at the way my tanned hand contrasted vividly against it. "How are you so pale?"

He caught my mouth with his again, kissing me for a few more moments before replying. "England is overcast most of the year, and I never go outside if I can help it. You'd be this pale too if you lived there. But enough," he said. "I'm not so English I want to talk about the weather when I have the most alluring woman on the seas in my arms."

"Listen, before this goes further," I said, "your family is still trying to kill me."

"It's their way of showing respect."

"I don't trust you or like you."

"Fine."

"We're not fucking, we're just..." I stopped. "No, this is a terrible idea." I stopped kissing him but I didn't move away.

"You're famous for terrible ideas," he countered.

"No, I'm famous for terrible ideas that work out." I slid my face down to his neck to nip at it. Underneath the recent dunking of seawater, he tasted... *fancy*. "I don't think there'd be any way to justify this."

"A pity," he whispered, sliding a hand under my shirt, but only to massage my very sore back. "You and I would make much better friends than enemies."

Awkwardly, we both stood, and returned to our respective beds. I contemplated all the reasons why being sensible was less of a virtue than people suggested, until sleep found me once more. This time, at least, I had no dreams.

22

———

The next morning, the decks were busy with preparations for bamboozling the navy. Everyone that wasn't going to be taking part in my high risk pantomime was sailing the ship, looking either incredibly jealous or incredibly relieved. I was at the helm, trying to not let the sight of Commodore St Stephen barking orders aboard my boat make me feel too churlish.

I was failing.

"Here." Something landed on the navigation maps next to me. I choked on my breakfast rum.

Lysander lifted a pale eyebrow. "Asleep at the wheel?"

"I was concentrating," I sniped, neglecting to mention that I had been concentrating on my drink. I dropped my flask to my side and picked up the bracelet he had tossed at me. "What's this?"

"An amulet that will let me communicate with you while you're down below." He held up his wrist to show off a matching one. It was both simple and gaudy, coloured clay beads interspersed with a few discoloured copper ones. The clay beads had fresh carvings on them, unfamiliar symbols, filled in with black ink.

"Really?" I scrunched up my nose. "They look like something out of Val's costume stash."

"It was, I just... improved it. And you're right, they need a little something extra." He flourished a small knife. "A little blood."

"You've got to be joking." I stepped away from him. "How are these meant to help us today, anyway?"

"Look," Lysander started, in an infuriatingly pleasant tone. "You're almost certainly feeling sour that you can't see the show." That wasn't why I was feeling sour but I was definitely disappointed about that. "This way I can show it to you without any risk."

I grunted, adjusting the course of the ship slightly.

"How do I know you won't do what your pa did to Elspeth with her ugly necklaces?"

Lysander snorted. "I'm not that powerful." He paused for a second, then his elegant shoulders shrugged. "Yet. Besides, it's a bracelet, not a manacle. You can fling it in the ocean whenever you want."

I held the bracelet gingerly, then whistled. "Dauntless!"

A few seconds later, I was answered by an ear splitting shriek, followed by a thumping of feathered wings. Dauntless the red parrot settled on the map, and nipped at my fingers.

"Ow, quit it." I yanked them back. "Can we add finding a way to let him talk while he's a parrot to the magical to-do list?"

Dauntless screamed and flapped his enormous wings, with zero dignity, but great presence.

"Or preferably remove the parrot curse," I amended.

"Duly noted." Lysander sounded uninterested in either prospect.

"Listen, Dauntless. Magic bracelets that let us talk," I held up mine, and grabbed Lysander by the wrist to show him his. "Something fucky happens, can you..."

Dauntless clicked his beak menacingly, then squawked at me before flying off.

"Feel better now that you have a parrot as back up?" Lysander picked up the knife again. I held out my arm, and he nicked the soft flesh just below the elbow gently, catching the startlingly red rivulet on the bracelet, and rubbing a thin sheen of the blood across the beads, before doing the same to his bracelet.

"I trust that parrot with my life and he hasn't let me down yet." I watched him nick his own soft pale arm and paint both bracelets with the blood.

"Well," he said, handing me one of the two blood stained pieces of arcane jewellery, "I hope you give as much credence to my own perfect record." With his bracelet in place, he tilted my head up for a kiss before I realised what he was doing, pressing his pale lips against mine, gripping my jaw with fingers still sticky with our mingled blood. Smirking, he sauntered off.

The commodore approached. Judging from the expression on his face he'd seen the end of the exchange. "How did he do that without getting stabbed?"

Commodore St Stephen looked almost as pristine as the day I met him, but not even his best efforts could get a navy outfit that fitted him perfectly, and we didn't have enough starch on board to get it as stiff as a plank of wood. He also wasn't wearing his stupid little white wig yet, so he still looked handsome—though not as handsome as he was before he shaved the beard.

The note of jealousy in his voice, however, made him much hotter.

"Got me jewellery."

"Jewellery," he repeated, sounding disbelieving.

"Covered in blood." I held up my wrist. "My favourite kind."

A flicker of a smile ghosted across the commodore's face before it smoothed into the smooth lines of the stringent authoritarian I'd met marooned on the British Navy's supply island. "Everyone is as prepared as they can be," he informed me. "And I will take this last opportunity to register my discomfort with these actions."

"Your discomfort is duly noted, but I refuse to be captured a minute before I have to be, so we'll be doing this my way."

"How do you know I won't sell you out?" St Stephen asked, his question as low as a breath. He stepped in and lowered his head so his mouth was level with my ear. "How do you know that once you are locked down below and I have the navy on board, that I won't simply hand you and your crew over?"

I breathed in deeply. Maybe he mistook it for fear, but I just wanted to smell him, his deeply masculine scent of the sea, ink, linen, sweat, and now even rum. I wanted him to press his whole body against me, not just his lips against my mouth. I tilt my head, letting his lips run down my neck before he caught himself, and stepped back.

"I believe in your honour," I said.

"You shouldn't," he said. "I've broken it before."

"No one's perfect. But I think everyone in this bargain— you, me, Grimstead— we're all waiting for someone else to blink first and shirk on the deal. There's little I have faith in, commodore, but I have faith in your honour."

He let out a ragged sigh. He sounded so tormented. I wanted to fuck it out of him but there wasn't the time and he probably wouldn't let me.

"How far away are we, captain?"

"White sails on the horizon." I pointed at a bright blob. The navy patrol, beyond which was less than a three hour sail to Port Elizabeth. "I guess this is now a navy vessel, commodore."

23

———

Despite my discomfort at locking myself in my own brig and handing the key to Sebastian, who was in my opinion the only fine looking figure in a navy red coat, there was a spring in my step as I threw myself down on the bench-slash-bed in the cell. If this wasn't a disaster, it was going to be sensationally entertaining. I wanted to get a good laugh in before things got deadly in Port Elizabeth.

In the cell opposite me, Elspeth rasped as she laboured to breathe, while in the larger cell taking up the rest of the brig, was everyone who was too piratical to disguise as navy or rescued merchant was locked up as part of my nefarious crew. The brig was probably the most honest part of this whole ship, ironically enough.

"I hope you're right about the commodore, cap'n," Smith said.

"I am," I replied confidently. "And if I'm wrong, we do what we always do."

"Shoot them all?"

"Damn right. You all have your guns hidden?" Affirmative

murmurs came from them. "Then we're grand. We mopped the floor with the navy yesterday."

I leaned back against the hull of the ship, which creaked and moaned comfortingly. The sound of home. After a few seconds, I pulled Lysander's bracelet out of my pocket and slipped it over my wrist.

Nothing happened.

Lysander? I thought, feeling silly for even thinking he might hear me.

Oh, you decided to trust me. His voice was in my head, with so much smugness it set my teeth on edge. *I knew your curiosity would win out over any sense of self preservation. Luckily for you, I was being honest. The commodore says we're about half an hour away from meeting the navy ship. You should take a nap. You didn't get enough sleep last night.*

I never get enough sleep, I retorted mentally. *I do my best work when I'm pushed to the edge.*

He was probably right, though. I should have dozed, but instead I spent the longest half hour of my life going through every possible way this scenario could go wrong and how I could react. People think I'm just impulsive but when I have time, I do like to plan. It gives me more options to be impulsive with.

Finally, Lysander's voice popped into my brain again. *Captain, are you awake? It's show time.*

In my mind's eye, I saw the deck of the ship and people on it. I wasn't getting any other senses, just visuals. *Am I seeing what you're seeing?*

Yes, came Lysander's reply. He sounded the same in my head as he did out loud, smooth and aristocratic, with a hint of sardonic laughter lurking at the edge of his words.

Why can't I hear what's going on?

Because I didn't have a lot of time to make the magic bracelets, he replied. *Now shhhh. Here they come.*

The navy boarded my ship. I gritted my teeth as they marched across the gangplanks and were solemnly saluted by a gaggle of pirates in navy uniforms, led by the commodore, whose face was as strict as I'd ever seen it.

I had, foolishly, allowed myself to forget what the commodore was when he was in his element. I had grown so used to him being on the defensive around me that seeing him at his apex made my stomach grow cold. Here was the predator that hunted me and my kind across the seas. The one that I had bargained for my life with when I was marooned on that island. These naval sailors he greeted had likely never met him him, but within minutes, I watched them start to follow his orders.

Lysander was also stepping forward and introducing himself. From the handshakes and respectful nods he received, I guessed his name carried weight too. I struggled to catch glimpses of my crew, performing their naval roles admirably, even though half of them were women with bound chests and fake beards.

Good news, Flint, they've bought our ruse and commodore isn't even letting them take a peep at you. Says prisoners aren't a spectacle, and if they're so keen, they can ask for shore leave to come witness the trial.

From what I could see, the naval captain and a few of his lieutenants were arguing with the commodore. There was an unexpected stab of warmth near my heart region. Ugh. What was that? It wasn't affection, was it? Why couldn't the commodore sit in a neat little box like I wanted him to? I was ready to put him back in the enemy box and then he did something nice like that.

He probably just didn't want me to shoot my mouth off.

Are they leaving? I asked impatiently, as the red coats moved slowly back in the direction of the gangplank.

Yes, yes. It's a lot of formalities now.

I yanked off the bracelet, cutting off whatever Lysander was about to say.

"Job done, mates, they fell for it hook, line and sinker," I told the crew in the brig with me. "The commodore and the wizard are just waving them off the boat now."

"I don't know what I expected when I signed on to sail with you." Sharky's voice was brimming with eagerness. "But this is even better than daring battles."

"Don't encourage her to get too clever," Smith muttered, then louder, he added, "but 'twas a good ruse, captain, and we saved a lot of the crew this way."

I didn't get a chance to reply because just then, the brig lit up with an unnatural purple glow. A rasp like a dinghy across dry sand pulled our attention.

Elspeth was sitting up, glowing, her hair floating around her in the purple light. When she spoke, it was in the same terrible rasp that we had just heard.

"So you are here then," the thing that was controlling Elspeth said. "I'm surprised. I had expected you to save your own skin. And you even brought Commodore St Stephen and my son."

I growled. Adrenaline flooded me. How *dare* he keep getting into spaces that were supposed to be safe? I was glad the cells separated us because I suspect I would have done Elspeth real harm trying to shake Magnus out of her.

"You can have them back." My knuckles were white as my fingers curled around the bars. "They're not great company,

Grimstead. I'm just here for my friend, and then we can be out of each others' hair."

"Moor your boat at the low market docks, on Pier Seventeen. Lysander can settle it with the harbourmaster. We will meet at the chapel of Saint Lucia. Both the commodore and my son will know the way."

"If Val isn't there, unharmed, I will kill everyone that turns up," I told him, my gaze boring into Elspeth's violet eyes. Hatred for Magnus burned through me like a bad batch of rum. Her burned lips twisted into a smile.

"I have no interest in her. I want my son, the commodore, and *you*."

With that, the light extinguished. Elspeth fell limply back onto her bed.

24

Val made me keep all my emergency supplies in one place and once again, I was thankful as fuck for her forethought. Yanking the chest out from behind a pile of silks piled up in the solid wood wardrobe in my cabin, I threw open the lid and began to prepare.

I wore my best set of boots for running. They were also the pair with the secret pockets so I could hide a straight razor and a set of lockpicks. I buckled a stiletto sheath to my outer left thigh—it was my off hand but it'd be a bigger surprise. I'd be wearing loose sailor's pants, since it'd be easier for running, and if you layer on enough scarves around your waist, no one notices the slit that runs all the way through the layers right to the thigh. Val says it's what the fancy ladies do with their big gowns, except they've got pockets tied on for whatever it is they need. Perfume or hand-kerchiefs, she said. They'd be better off carrying stilettos, in my opinion. I'm sure 'men of quality' are just as handsy, if not more so, than the ruffian lads.

I was so distracted by my thoughts of arming posh ladies

and tying on my distraction waist sashes that when my cabin door opened I jumped a mile.

"I did knock, captain," the commodore said, as he stepped inside. He was still dressed in his navy clothes, those tight white trousers showing off every curve of his shapely legs. Unfortunately his blue coat swished in the way of his 'mast' area, as if he knew right where I'd look.

"I suppose you're going to keep that get up on until we arrive, aren't you?" I said.

"It makes little sense not to, seeing as I am returning to my home and my rank." He was more subdued saying that than I would have expected him to be. He took a breath. "May I have a private moment, captain?"

"Aye, but only if you lose the wig. I won't talk to you when you're wearing that ridiculous thing."

His mouth flattened into a line but the long suffering look in his eyes revealed more amusement than genuine annoyance as he shut the door behind him with one hand, and pulled the powdered white wig from his head with the other.

"You look much better," I told him, as I slid my second favourite set of knives into my belt sheaths. I was expecting to lose them but that didn't mean I was going to take inferior knives into what might be a fight.

"Compliments from you are as meaningless as ever."

"And yet you're blushing."

"Are you...hiding things on your person?"

"It's your keen sense of perception that propelled you through the ranks, isn't it?" I grinned. "I'm not going into whatever this is unprepared. Are you going to rat me out?" I shrugged into a fancy waistcoat with poison hidden in the lining.

"I'm going to follow the law, and I will ensure—" He

stopped and took a deep breath. His jaw clenched and he looked at me with those eyes that seemed to be drowning so often when they found mine. "I came to thank you, captain."

My hand stilled on the buttons. "Is that right?"

"Yes. You have shown me—" He took another deep breath. His hands gripped the back of a wooden chair so tightly his knuckles were white. "You saved my life, and furthermore, you protected me from the violence of your compatriots even when it didn't serve any immediate purpose for you."

"You know how I like to keep people on their toes." Was it the uniform that was having this effect on him? In the last few days it had seemed like he'd almost been relaxed at times, and now he was retreating back into his shell. "Besides, it was all self interest. I told you that."

"I cannot defy the systems of justice you have violated," the commodore said with great seriousness. "If your self interest was to buy my honour, surely you must know by now you have failed." He did not meet my eyes. Did he feel bad selling me out to the noose? Well, he should.

Luckily, that wasn't what I was talking about.

"Oh I'm smarter than that, I'd never bank on you taking my side over the law," I unbuttoned the waistcoat I'd just done up and sauntered over to him. Standing on the far side of the chair, I lifted my hand and put it on his smooth face, freshly shaven. He looked at me, startled by my proximity.

"I told you I just want to fuck you."

"You can't still be serious about that." He pulled back from my hand like it burned.

"Last chance, commodore. No one back home has to know."

I put my hands on either side of his on the back of the

chair, leaning towards him, tilting my face up. He was taller than me and with the chair between us, I wasn't going to be able to reach him. He was going to have to come to me.

I expected him to be annoyed, but not nearly the level of annoyed that I actually elicited. His jaw clenched so tightly his lips went white. A vein in his neck I had never noticed before stood out as it throbbed with what I can only assume was his elevated heart rate.

"Everything is a game to you." He barely got the words out between his teeth. The solid heels of my boots hit the deck with a thud as I quit leaning forward, but did not look away from his heated glare.

"Not true, and you know that." I smacked my palm against the arm of the chair. "This has been all business. I didn't bring this many people here on a—" I nearly said *fool's errand* but I swallowed the words, because the name of my old ship was still a sore point, "—a suicide mission. I've played it smart. I didn't play it like you would. But we're nearly there and we're going to make the hand off just as arranged, and then I'm probably going to die so why are you so up in arms that I'm trying to have a little fun before that happens?"

"You nearly died *yesterday*." Commodore St Stephen yelled the words so loudly that I stepped back in surprise. "You didn't catch that second gun, and you could have died."

"Today, tomorrow, does it matter to you?" I raked my fingers through my hair in genuine exasperation. The man looked like a pot that'd been on the boil for too long, or a tavern of rowdy sailors on the cusp of the mood turning.

"Unless...it *does* matter to you?" I stepped back to him and kicked the treacherous chair out of the way. Surprised, he let it go, and it made a brief racket as it tumbled across the cabin.

"You're important to a lot of people," he said, his eyes fixed on mine. "You make an impact on people."

"Looks like I've made an impact on you." I laid my hand on the brocade waistcoat under the heavy naval coat and ran my hand over it, following it up to his shoulders where it turned to soft linen.

"I didn't think you were capable of such gross understatements." His hands hovered awkwardly beside me, but he did not pull away from my touch. His eyes flickered shut as a pained expression crossed his face. "I can't save you in Port Elizabeth. Do you understand?"

"I must pay for my life of crime?"

"It's simply—simply not how it works. There are systems. I have responsibilities and—"

"Oh, untwist your breeches. I don't for a fucking second think you're going to save me." I snorted. "I like to do the saving of folks around these parts anyway."

He didn't say anything at all, and I made myself keep my mouth shut to see which way he'd jump. Would he just storm out the door?

Why was I stirring him up like this anyway? Last chance for it, I suppose.

His hands gently wrapped around my wrists, my two outstretched hands still resting on the front of his chest. I expected him to push my hands away, but instead, he fanned his fingers over my hands where they rested. The calloused, sailor's hands that had sewn me up after the battle. He was touching me for no reason other than he wanted to.

I didn't have to fight myself from saying something stupid because every word evaporated from my mind in surprise.

"I am who I am." His shoulders sagged, his eyes never leaving mine. "And that means I can't, even though..."

He dropped his hands from mine and turned away.

"Even though what?" I shouted, grabbing his shoulder. Thank god there was no one there to see me pouncing after a man. "Even though you...*want to?*"

His shoulders tensed, and he half turned back, locking eyes with me, eyes burning in a way I had never seen before. He took a deep breath.

"Captain! Commodore!" The cabin door flew open and Sharky skidded in.

The commodore and I both leapt apart as if jolted by lightning.

"Mister Lysander says to stop fighting and come out on deck as soon as possible. We're in the harbour now." Sharky blinked at us. "Sorry, was I interrupting?"

To my eternal credit, I did not keelhaul Sharky.

25

The bustling markets of lower Port Elizabeth weren't too different from what I was used to, aside from the regular patrols of navy officers, the intimidating wall of the fort built into the cliffside, and the fact that all the buildings mostly matched. Otherwise, it was all common folk in workaday clothes shouting, laughing, and sweating in the brilliant noonday sun.

A beautiful day for a hostage exchange, I reflected as our party strolled through the markets, following the commodore's lead. Blue skies, wisps of white cloud, and a nice sea breeze. On the one hand, it seemed a shame to waste it on such bullshit, but on the other, if it was stormy, visibility would be rubbish and my gunpowder would get wet.

Our group consisted of myself, the commodore, Lysander, and half a dozen crew members experienced in escaping on land. Dauntless was keeping tabs on us from the sky. Back on the ship, I had left Sebastian and Smith in charge.

"When Val comes back, she's in charge. She makes the final call on when to leave. Dauntless will be too..." I checked that the parrot was out of earshot. "He'll be too upset to make good decisions." Smith nodded knowingly, puffing on his pipe. "If Val and I don't come back, it's your call. The two of you are in in charge. Rescue us, blow this place to Davy Jones' locker, or just put this all to your rudder. Do what's best for the crew."

Smith had readily agreed. I could count on him to make the hard calls when it came down to it. Sebastian looked unhappy with the responsibility I placed on him and protested.

"You seemed ready enough to pick up Val's duties at the Last Doubloon," I reminded him. "Besides, Val trusted you, and someone needs to represent her people. Smith speaks for the pirates, but you speak for the Pleasure Emporium."

With my responsibilities accounted for, I landed in the heart of Kill Magpie Flint territory.

Our merry little band had climbed out of the lower markets and was now in an area with cobbled streets and glass shopfronts. There were flowers growing in the box planters outside the windows and the people walking around us got a lot cleaner.

"This is the nice part of town, is it?" I eyed a shopfront that seemed to exclusively display brass nautical instruments and time pieces. "I can tell we're bringing down the tone."

I wasn't being flippant either. The other people on the street, mostly ladies in large skirts and tight bodices, gave us a wide berth, even as their curious gazes lingered longer than was polite.

"How do you normally keep the riff raff out?" I pulled out a dagger, twirling it impressively without looking, and then sheathed it again, to the horrified shrieks of the ladies watching.

"Force," the commodore replied, his voice deadpan. "That's enough, Flint. This way."

He turned down a narrow sidestreet. The buildings here were all very small shopfronts for niche items such as hats, fine china and books. Above the shops were residences. It was very clean. Nice, tidy people with quiet lives must live there, I thought, who would never in their lives imagine pirates traipsing past their doors on their way to a prisoner exchange. I flicked my eyes to the roofs to check for an ambush, but it was all clear apart from a familiar bright red parrot doing his best to fly unobserved alongside us.

The street ended in a sharp turn upwards. On the corner was a small church with a lovely garden planted out the front, complete with English grass.

"This is the Santa Lucia chapel," the commodore announced, as we stopped outside the low stone wall that surrounded the chapel and its gardens.

I immediately grabbed Lysander and put my pistol to his head. "Grimstead," I shouted. "Come out, come out, wherever you are."

"*Hey*," Lysander protested.

"It's okay, I still like you," I murmured in his ear. "Just play along."

From the dark doorway of the chapel, Haddrick and Mercer goons swarmed out like ants. There probably weren't more than a dozen, but they were big and the churchyard was small. Last to emerge from the sanctified darkness was Magnus Grimstead, with his bony hand on Val's arm.

In my enormous relief, I almost let my grip on Lysander drop. Val looked no worse for wear than when she had been taken. She was wearing the same clothes down to her enormous spectacles, had no visible injuries, and wore a look of quiet disdain on her face as though she were merely inconvenienced by the whole ordeal. When her eyes landed on me, they lit up with relief. I gave her a small, bloodthirsty smile.

"This is a nice part of town," I told Grimstead. "It'd be a shame to spill blood all over it. So let's do this neatly. I'll send over the commodore. You send over Val. Then I'll come over with your son. Sound fair?"

"Your reasoning being that my son is the most valuable part of this exchange to me?" The old man laughed, a wheezy sound. "How charming that you think so. But I agree to the terms."

Lysander grumbled unhappily and I exchanged a look with the commodore. I jerked my head at him.

He walked through the church gate slowly and stood beside Magnus Grimstead. The wizard looked him up and down. Meeting some kind of approval, he released Val's arm and shoved her towards us. With far more hurry than the commodore, Val rushed across the garden and was enveloped in a gaggle of pirates.

"Maggie!" Val grabbed my arm. "You can't go with him! I don't know what they're all up to but they will use you for ill—"

I let Lysander go and gave my best friend a quick hug. "I know. Don't worry about me. I'll find some way out. Get back to the ship. You're in charge. I love you, Val." I handed her my pistol.

"If you don't start walking in three seconds, we'll start shooting," Magnus announced in a convivial tone, as if simply drawing our attention to the finer points of the architecture.

"What's the hurry? Can you smell the Grim Reaper's

breath?" I grabbed Lysander's arm and dragged him towards the church.

"I can walk on my own, you know."

"Yeah but I'm not going to get shot just because you're mad you're not your dad's favourite."

We crossed into the walled garden and stood in front of Magnus and the commodore, surrounded by Haddrick and Mercer's heavies. I looked over my shoulder. My people were still standing there. Dammit, they had instructions.

"Go!" I shouted, irritated. "Get out of here!"

For a second nobody moved. Hands hovered near weapons. Val's eyes looked as mutinous as I had ever seen them, twins of my own - we'd learned them in the same place.

Finally, they moved, even Val, backing down the side street and out of sight. Relief and terror washed over me at once and I turned back towards my captors. Before I could ask what next, something heavy hit me on the back of the head and everything went dark.

26

I woke up in a room where every item looked more valuable than everything I owned combined. Specifically, I woke up in a plush bed that felt like it would be extremely comfortable to sleep on in normal circumstances. Right now though, my arms and legs hurt from lying in the unconscious sprawl I had landed in when some goon had simply hurled me down like a sack of sugar.

Mercifully, I wasn't tied up.

I checked my belongings. The knives were, as expected, gone. Even the stiletto on my thigh and the straight razor in my boot. I still had my waistcoat with the hidden pockets of poison, however, and they hadn't found the lockpicks hidden in my boots when they nabbed the straight razor. Wonderful.

Rubbing the back of my throbbing head, I looked around. The room was large by my standards, containing the fancy canopy bed, a lounging couch of the sort that Val liked, an armchair, a wash stand with a basin, a bookcase and a small cabinet. Only one wall had windows. When I peered out, I saw I was on the third floor, facing the back of the property: I couldn't see the harbour and if I tried to climb out the window, there were plenty of people about who'd see me. If I could even climb down three storeys.

Of course, there was a lot of drapery...so I had options.

There was also all the usual rich people clutter: vases, little statues, knickknacks and other *things*. In my line of work, they were more often than not simply projectiles. Imagine taking my knives but leaving me this marble bookend. I gave it a heft in my hand. It'd do nicely as a weapon.

Naturally, I tried the door. It was locked. Picking them right away would play my hand before I was prepared. I knocked instead.

"Anyone out there?" I called. "I want to report violence and kidnapping. Some fucker hit me over the back of the head and brought me here. I thought this town was one of law and order!"

I heard scrambling and a hushed conversation, followed by one set of footsteps hurrying away.

"Fetching the boss, huh?" I got no reply. I guess they knew better than to leave the chatty ones. Or maybe they were too green to be up for banter with a pirate.

I threw myself down on the chaise longue, making sure my dirty boots were on the nicely upholstered seat, and waited, idly placing bets with myself about who they'd send.

I lost all of my bets when the door opened and the wall-like frame of Wilfred Haddrick appeared in the room.

"Thank god you're not wearing that hat," I said, without moving from my recline. "Between your shoulders and ego, and my ego and intellect, I don't think the hat would've fit in the room."

One half of the Caribbean's biggest shipping empire stared at me as the cogs in his brains turned. Clearly he didn't remember the ridiculous hat of overcompensation he was wearing when we met for the first and, until now, only time.

"What can I do for you, Wilfred?" I asked pleasantly, and gestured at him to sit down in one of the other chairs in the room.

He growled. "You're not going to treat this like you're in charge," he barked. A vein in his forehead pulsed.

"You're right." I swung my legs to the ground and sat up. Holding my hands up peaceably, I smiled at him, the most charming smile I could muster. It didn't work. I probably showed too many teeth. Val said I did that when I was mad.

"You're coming to the ball tonight." He jabbed a finger at me. "We're going to show everyone we've caught you, and that Haddrick and Mercer have made the seas safe for everyone."

"Is that how you ask all the ladies to the ball? You're normally supposed to say things like please, and would you, and maybe call me beautiful."

"We are not going together." The man's brain finally caught up to the conversation I was having. "I'm just informing you."

"Who am I going with then? Is it Mr Mercer?"

"There's no Mr Mercer. It's *Miss* Mercer and she's coming with me." He looked pleased with this. Either Miss Mercer was very attractive, or what he lacked in understanding of social interactions he made up for in understanding of business. "You're going in the cage."

"That sounds unpleasant," I said conversationally.

"It is." He covered the distance between us and picked me up off the chaise like I was a rag doll. Had he been Sebastian, or the commodore, or Dauntless, it would have been attractive, but Haddrick was just a thug. "You've made everything a complete fucking pain. Angie won't marry me until we get rid of you, and it turns out not even the fucking commodore could bring you down. But we've got you now and if you don't behave, I'm going to make you miserable."

"Counterpoint." I hung like a dead weight in his grip, keeping my eyes level with his, forcing him to keep expending energy on holding me up. "You put me down now and I don't bite your nose off. If you lay a hand on me again, of any sort, and I'll serve your dick and balls to Angie on a platter and we'll see how she feels about marrying you then."

His grip on my arms intensified. I drove my foot into his balls.

Big men drop heavily. Even an absolute bulwark like Wilfred Haddrick goes down when kicked in the kraken by an expert.

The doors flew open and the guards came in. I was back to lounging on my chaise and Haddrick was on the floor, spitting and cursing.

"You should do whatever Miss Mercer thinks is best," I told the flunkies casually, as they looked between their weapons, me and one of their bosses on the floor. From the way they backed away, I could tell that Miss Mercer was definitely the business end of Haddrick and Mercer.

Gathering himself, Haddrick pulled himself to his feet and dragged himself from the room. Red faced with anger and pain, he looked back and said, "In two days you'll be dead."

"Maybe," I replied. "But I'll make sure you have a permanent memento to remember me by."

The door slammed.

Wildred Haddrick never even noticed he'd lost one of his daggers while he'd been on the floor.

27

_____

While I waited for the ball to get under way, I imagined how the conversation went between Mercer, Haddrick and Grimstead and whatever other lackeys were in the room that resulted in the action plan of '*Let's display Magpie Flint in a cage at the centre of a ball like some sort of exotic creature.*' I can only assume they thought it would be humiliating for me, but, obviously they didn't know me very well. There's usually only one way to show off a captured pirate and that involves a hanging. Sitting alive and well in a room full of easily frightened rich people was a considerable step up from that.

Maybe rich people thought being looked at was some kind of punishment. If that was the case, it didn't explain why they puffed and preened the way they did. I'd have to ask Val if maybe they all had some kind of humiliation kink.

"The thing is," I remarked to one of the young navy officers unfortunate enough to be stationed by my cage, "rich people think I should be embarrassed because I don't have anything worth looking at, that's my theory. They have expensive clothing, perfumes, jewelry, in-bred chins, all that stuff. They think they're saying to everyone, look at this bitch with no money, we caught her, and you can all go look at her. But they've got it all wrong. Normally I spend all my time thinking about how to get into places like this. They've just planted me right here. Anyway, I love being the centre of attention," I continued, while the rookie tried to stare straight ahead. "You think I'd have become the most famous pirate in the Caribbean if I didn't? Rich people are not good at thinking about anyone other than themselves, that's the problem with them. It doesn't make them good at strategy,"

"Can you shut up?" the navy rookie whispered.

"Absolutely not," I said. "Well. Maybe. Do you think you can get me something with alcohol in it?"

The poor sap looked like he was thinking about it when Lysander's voice rang out behind him.

"Wright, don't give the pirate any alcohol, it'll probably cost you your job. Also, I heard your commodore was looking for you. Don't worry, I can handle the prisoner. Run along."

Lysander waited until the navy's greenest sailor scurried off. "Are you going to scare all of the commodore's men, Flint?"

"Just the wimps." I settled comfortably on the cushion my literal gilded cage had been outfitted with. "Really, talking is all I can do from here."

He laughed, and couldn't argue. I couldn't reach anyone through the bars, as there was a second cage enclosing the first—I was told that something with large tusks had been in there previously and the second cage was installed after someone blessed with more gold than brains had gotten too close and been gored. Now, it was serving to keep the quality at a wide berth from the pirate.

"I hope you told them this was a ridiculous idea," I said to Lysander.

"I warned them you would cause trouble, but my father is confident he's more than capable of matching it." Lysander shrugged. He was dressed in an impressive blue silk coat embroidered with gold threads. The blue matched his eyes so perfectly, it had to have been dyed especially. Underneath I caught sight of a contrasting gold vest with blue embroidery, and a white shirt underneath that. His trousers matched his coat, and so did his shoes.

He looked incredible. I felt terribly under-dressed but at least I looked the part of a notorious pirate.

"It's ridiculous for them," I replied cheerfully. "I'm going to tell so many tales they don't want told."

"Oh, please do, I'd love nothing more than for you to ruin my father but I fear you will find no sympathetic listeners in this audience, Flint." He shrugged delicately. "To them pirates are all scum and thieves. They won't even believe you about the magic. Speaking of which, some good news for you. My father and I successfully unlinked me from your ship this afternoon. I'm free from you. You're free from me."

"That's two major victories today. I'm doing well."

Lysander's smile looked more bitter than it should have. "Watch your back, Flint. I think your victories are about to run out."

"AND THEN I SAID, IT'S THE HAT. I CAN'T TAKE ANYONE WITH such an overly large hat seriously, and I shot him," I told a crowd of Port Elizabeth's finest, recounting my victory over

Wilfred Haddrick the previous week in the battle of the Last Doubloon.

"Clearly, you did not succeed in killing him," sniffed an older woman who was suffering from a severe deficiency in chin.

"Aye, keenly observed, madame," I replied. "Alas, my shot was stray of its mark by a few hairs, due to the bucking of the seas beneath us. But killing him personally was never my aim, though I would have liked that feather in my own reasonably sized cap very much. You see, it was all a distraction, because at that moment, the cannonades fired again— and this time they took out one of Mercer and Haddrick's ships."

"Once again, t's *Haddrick and Mercer,*" growled a young man with an absurdly perfect nose.

I was revising the story as I was going along, but I wasn't about to try and sell the creme de la creme of Port Elizabeth on the notion that Haddrick and Mercer were allied with wizards. I would count myself lucky if I could convince them that they were dicks. I was also deliberately getting their name wrong about half the time just to wind them up.

"You retook the cannon gauntlet!" gasped an older man with a monocle clutched in his left eyesocket. "That is dastardly. Highly lax on their part not to expect it, however."

"Never assume your opponent is stupid. It gets people killed," I replied smugly. "So at that point, I make my farewell to Wilfred Haddrick, and dive into the ocean, and when I reach my ship, do you know what I see him doing? He's fleeing. Haddrick's flagship is fleeing, not even signalling a retreat and cutting off his own fleet."

"That seems extremely unlikely," cried a younger woman

whose own lack of chin indicated she was related to the older woman.

"Then how do you explain the fact that only the flagship made it back?"

"You and your bloodthirsty, murderous pirate compatriots killed them all, obviously," the chinless old woman sneered, snapping her fan shut.

I laughed. "No money in killing people, lady. Give it another few days and our ransom notices will arrive. You'll find they are alive, and you can get them back for a reasonable price." I shrug. "And if they don't come back, maybe Mercer and Haddrick were too flint skinned to pay for them."

"For the last bloody time, it's *Haddrick and Mercer*."

A tinkling bell was rung and a dance announced. My audience drifted away, casting looks at me ranging from the curious to the furious. Only one figure remained behind, a young girl in a dress that looked like it weighed more than she did, her hair immaculately pinned to her head in an elaborate arrangement I doubted even Val could mimic. Her wide green eyes shone with excitement as they stared at me.

"Hello!" she said. "I'm so pleased to meet you, Captain Flint. I've heard all the stories about you."

"Kid, even I haven't heard all the stories about me."

She laughed like I had said something genuinely funny, instead of being tired and flippant.

"Who are you? Are you even old enough to be here?" I asked.

"I'm Georgiana Weatherby," she replied, curtsying. I had to assume it was perfect, the kid looked like the sort to have it down pat, but of course no one had ever curtsied to me before. "My father is the Governor of the local area. And of course I'm old enough to be here, I'm sixteen. I certainly wasn't going to miss a chance to meet my hero."

"Your... hero?"

"You!" Georgiana replied with great excitement. "I have to keep it a secret, but I admire you greatly. Your independence, your competence, your great many skills. But more than anything, I admire your refusal to be bound by society's expectations."

I noted the wistfulness in her last statement. "Are they trying to get you to do something you don't want to do?"

Her whole body drooped, like a wilted flower. "My father wishes me to marry Aristides Grimstead."

"Oh fuck off," I said. "Fuck that. The hell you will. You're too young to be marrying anyone, let alone that freak."

When I was sixteen, I was already running my own crew of rum smugglers, but I think Georgiana had led a much more sheltered life than I had.

"What should I do?" Georgiana held the bars of the outer cage, leaning in as far as she could. "My father controls my whole life. I have nowhere to go. I have no skills. I have no friends that would not immediately betray me to him. I don't even have my own money."

"Listen, kid, Georgiana—I'm probably going to die tomorrow, being executed for piracy and all, but *you* don't have to be a prisoner. Don't have money? You're joking, right? You're *wearing* enough money right now to live a comfortable life somewhere else. You've got a choice between certain hell or the unknown. Always pick the unknown. Just pack some things, wait for your moment and then leave. You don't know what'll happen but you're choosing the chance of something good over something definitely bad, right? That's my philosophy anyway." I shrugged. "No point going the direction I know is going to be bad. Might as well go a different way. It might be worse, but at least I tried."

Georgiana listened to me seriously. I felt like if she had a pen and some paper, she'd be writing it all down. "Right."

"And," I said, leaning as close as I could, which wasn't very close at all, leading me again to wonder about what kind of creature they had tried to display here and how badly it had gone. "If you *do* end up having to marry a Grimstead or some other man you don't want to, sneak a knife in on your wedding night, then before he can lay a hand on you, and stab him right here. Are you looking? Right here." I pointed to my inner thigh. "Nice and deep. There's an artery. He'll bleed out in ten, fifteen seconds tops. Throw open the window, cradle his body and start screaming about an assassin. They might suspect but they'll never be able to prove it was you."

Georgiana had gone pale, but there was still a spark in her eyes."Are you saying I should *murder* him?" she whispered, sounding... probably more interested than she meant to.

"It's what he deserves for marrying someone who doesn't want to marry him. Look, your father's the governor, no one is going to - "

I was very suddenly cut off by an explosion somewhere else inside the house, immediately followed by frantic shouting.

28

"I think that's my signal to jump ship," I told Georgiana, stooping down to fish the lockpicks from my boots. I set to work on the lock of my cage—tricky, since I had to work back to front and I couldn't see the lock, but right now everyone was busy looking in some other direction, so I had to take what I could get.

"Can I help?" the governor's daughter asked, with perfect sincerity.

"Sure," I grunted, trying to hold the torque pick steady. "You're the lookout. If it looks like anyone is coming over here to deal with me, go and cry on them about how upset you are. You're worried about your hair. What will your father say? Something like that. Just keep talking."

"I can do that." She straightened up, her gaze swept the ballroom with the focus of a thief looking for her next mark. I had no time to ponder my strange new ally, concentrating instead on keeping my breath steady and hoping my fingers didn't sweat as I jiggled the rake pick, trying to get the last tumbler to fall in place...

It clicked.

Untangling my arms from the bars and breathing a sigh of relief, I ran up to the next lock, which was a lot simpler. The door swung open, placing me face to face with Georgiana.

"Which way out, kid?" She pointed to a wall of windows not far from us. "Very funny. I meant a door."

"You won't find one unguarded," she replied. "These face the gardens, there's no fence and you can follow the path straight down to the town and the harbour."

I looked around the room. The guests huddled down the end with the large fireplace and the musicians, surrounded by navy men and men in colours I didn't recognise. They weren't paying any attention to me. There was fighting some-where else in the house, judging by the shots and shouts.

A second later, several navy men came running into the room, helpfully declaring their intentions by pointing and shouting: "There she is!"

"Definitely time to go," I told Georgiana, and ran for the wall of tall windows. I had no idea how to open them, or even if they opened. Instead, I grabbed the bust of someone's illus-trious but ugly ancestor and heaved it through the glass and then threw myself after him.

Only to hit a soft, springy wall and be immediately thrown back into the room, landing on my ass on the polished hardwood floor.

"The fuck!" I shouted as the navy men reached me and grabbed me. They hauled me to my feet. I would've sworn on my ship that the window I tried to go out of sparkled with a purple sheen of light—clearly some sorcerous fuckery at play.

That bell tinkled again while I fought against my captors, and a woman's voice rang out in the hall.

"I'm terribly sorry for the interruption to our night of celebration." The woman's voice was commanding and steady, with a cool hint of promise. Promise of what? I don't know, but it was the kind of voice that made people with less willpower than me stick around to find out more. I tried to break a man's elbow and nearly succeeded. "We always anticipated that the most notorious pirate captain on the seas would be an exciting exhibit! But never fear—the intruders who came for her were thwarted, and no harm has come to any guest. I commend the fearless men of Commodore St Stephen and my house guard."

Calls of 'bravo' and applause broke out, haltingly at first, and then gaining momentum as the speaker encouraged them.

Who *was* this woman?

"Now you see why I was so eager to have you all here tonight to see for yourselves what a great task Haddrick and Mercer have accomplished in removing Captain Magpie Flint from the seas. Without her leadership, the remaining pirates will fall to petty factionalism and the navy will be easily able to pick them off. Naval trade is now the safest it has ever been, thanks to the work of myself and Mr Haddrick."

'Angie' Mercer, then. She did sound like she meant business. A pity I couldn't see her. I hope she wasn't as ridiculously dressed as her commercial counterpart.

"We will just tuck our troublesome pirate away, and then continue with the festivities. They will not be so foolish to try again tonight. Music! Drinks!"

The room transformed back into a party. The musicians

started playing on command, and servants marched in carrying drinks. Everyone had forgotten I was even there.

Everyone except my guards and the only two people in the room who liked me.

Georgiana looked at me with a frightened face as they dragged me past her and mouthed, "I'm sorry."

And Lysander Grimstead leaning near the door. He ran his eyes over me, lifted an eyebrow at me while directing a comment to my captors. "Careful. She looks like she's about to escape."

"What would you know about escaping," one of the navy men sneered.

"I *do* know you boys somehow let every single one of the pirates that attacked the house leave alive." Lysander laughed and took a long drink from his glass. He fixed me with a long stare and turned away.

As my captors returned me to my room-turned-prison, relief flooded through me. I mentally thanked Lysander. All my friends had survived, even though they didn't succeed in rescuing me.

And now I had my first impression of Angie Mercer, although I hadn't seen her. She seemed commanding and charming. What was she like up close and personal?

It turned out I didn't need to wait long to find out.

29

It was less than half an hour later, by my estimation, when the door opened again. I was marched down some plush corridors, with carpet on the floor and fancy paper on the walls. My destination was on the second floor. This room was what I imagine the phrase an 'elegantly appointed' drawing room (or tea room or receiving room) meant. I read that phrase in a book back when the nuns used to make me read books, but I never learned the difference between the functions. Instead, I marvelled at the luxury of having enough rooms to bother coming up with all those names for them. To me, it just looked like it was filled to the brim with expensive things by someone who knew how to display them with understated intimidation. The rich woman's equivalent of a heavily armed pirate swinging onto your ship and introducing themselves with a witty one liner and a rapier swish.

Sure, the rapier was an expensive vase of exotic flowers, but thinking that meant she was any less dangerous would be a deadly mistake.

And this was *definitely* a woman's room. There were *fresh* flowers in those expensive vases, no weapons on display and the large portrait about the crackling fireplace was of a woman too young and shapely to be anyone's mother or wife.

The guards shackled me to a heavy wooden chair when we got inside. It didn't match anything in the room, so I knew they brought it in just for me. Guards stood at the door and either side of me. I'd lost my lockpicks back in the ballroom but they were clearly taking no chances this time. They weren't navy men this time either. They wore a uniform I didn't recognise. The Mercer house guard that Angie had mentioned earlier, probably.

"Who are we waiting for?" I asked after a few minutes of silence. Nobody answered me. I sighed. "They really don't hire you lot for the conversation, do they?"

My eyes were drawn back to the portrait while we waited. Something about the woman's face kept catching my attention. No matter how long I stared at her, I couldn't figure it out. I'd never seen her before. So why did my gut scream that I knew her? Had I maybe glimpsed her at the ball?

At long last, the door opened and three figures swept in. Two I recognised at once: Magnus Grimstead, cutting a much more polished figure than I had last seen him. He was dressed in a resplendent purple outfit that was the height of fashion and walking with a smart walking cane that was as well polished as his bald head. Lysander followed him. The third person took me a second to recognise: she was of average height, but seemed taller because of her styled hair. She had a stubborn jaw, high cheekbones and her dark eyes felt like they missed nothing when they turned on me.

"Nice painting of you over there," I said, after a beat. "The artist really captured your air of menace. Your eyes say, *I may or may not eat a small child today.*"

The woman burst into laughter at this, unladylike, mirthful laughter, and it sent a shock through me. I shot a look at Lysander, but his gaze was fixed on the mystery woman, wearing the same kind of puzzlement I felt.

"Thank you, Magpie—may I call you Magpie?" Her lip quirked insincerely at me as she seated herself.

"Absolutely fucking not," I replied sweetly.

"I'm so glad to meet you at last," she continued, motioning for the Grimsteads to seat themselves on either side of her. Their three chairs were considerably more plush than mine and naturally, they weren't chained to them. "You've been dreadfully hard to get a hold of. I've had the navy, Haddrick and Mercer, and Magnus looking for you. I'm actually very impressed."

"You can kiss my ass," I bit back, though I was still more confused than angry. "So what the fuck is it you want from me?"

"This is so much more refreshing than dealing with people with manners," she remarked to the Grimsteads. "They'll insult you but take an eternity about it. Magpie just cuts to the chase."

"She really does," Lysander hummed. He leaned back in his seat, eyes fixed on the woman, but despite his casual posture, there was a tightness through the core of his body. The man was smart, I had to hand it to him. He knew he was amongst predators.

"I'll cut to the chase too," the woman said, ignoring Lysander's remark. "My name is Evangeline Mercer. I've inherited half of Haddrick and Mercer from my father and I intend to build on his work to build an even greater shipping empire. I won't bore you with my business plans."

"And you need me off the seas because you think I'm

some kind of rallying point for the pirates?" I shook the chains as loud as I could. "Listen, Angie. I don't know what's in the face powder you've caked on, but it's addling your thinking, all right?" She looked at me with a half smile that bordered on a smirk, but I wasn't sure posh ladies smirked. "Taking me off the seas isn't going to solve your pirate problem. Just between us, I'm not the big fish you think I am. I'm flattered you're such an admirer but I think you've greatly overestimated how much of a threat that I personally pose to your business."

Lysander looked at Evangeline for her response.

Evangeline and Magnus exchanged smug, knowing looks.

"You're right." Evangeline flashed me a dazzling smile, showing too many teeth. "You're not in my way, much. I made that up for all the lack-brain moneybags downstairs. There is, however, a reason I need you off the seas. And another reason I needed to meet you in person."

I looked between her and Magnus. "This is some fucked up magic shit, isn't it? You're going to do something weird with like... my blood, or my teeth or something."

Angie smiled again, reaching her arms up to start doing something with her hair. "In a way, yes."

I actually ran out of words at this point. I was used to arrogant people, violent people, sneaky people. This was the first time I had met *batshit insane rich people.*

A series of metallic clinks followed as hair pins hit the table. Evangeline lifted the elaborate hair style away, revealing it to be a wig. She stood up and set it on a little table, and continued removing pins from her hair until it fell from the simple braid and fanned out behind her in a dark curtain. With quick motions, she wiped the makeup from her face with a cloth and water from a basin, and walked around the table to where I sat.

"Look at me," she demanded, lowering herself so that her dress pooled around her and her face was eye level with mine.

"Are you going to hypnotise me?" I asked, half revolted, half afraid. Fuck, who knew at this point? Not me. I was off the map. Here there be dragons.

Without the tall hair and the exaggerated features of the makeup, she looked even more familiar. Her unbrushed hair was a dark mass around her face, dark eyes both jovial and dangerous.

I *knew* this face. *I knew this face.*

Lysander choked. "*Fuck.* That's not possible. That's —how?"

It was the smile.

The smile gave it away.

When she smiled, slow and with teeth, I recognised her.

30

She was me.

Or rather, she looked identical to me.

"Who the fuck *are* you?" I yelped, leaning back as far as I could go. "Why do you have my face?" I whipped round to Magnus Grimstead. "This is your sorcerous bullshit, isn't it?"

"Not this time, pirate." He looked faintly amused. "The answer is as prosaic as it is unlikely."

"Even if Magnus could metamorphose faces at will, how could he possibly transform anyone into you?" Evangeline Mercer asked from my face—or what my face would look like if I'd lived a life of comfort. "He's never seen you, let alone studied you up close."

"Someone saw me well enough to draw that wanted poster," I replied. Evangeline tilted her head and arched a well plucked eyebrow at me pityingly. My stomach fell into a strange freefall with the realisation. "That was you. They drew *you*."

Why was it so cutting that it wasn't even my face on my wanted posters? That the woman who hunted me had posed for them seemed extra treacherous... But it still didn't explain why she looked identical to me.

"All right, so it's not magic. Then what? We're identical twins separated at birth?" My wild suggestion sat heavily in the air for several seconds.

"A proposition that is as unlikely as it is true." Evangeline broke the silence. Lysander openly stared in amazement. Magnus continued to look amused. "That is to say, entirely."

"You're telling me we're twins. You and I." I cackled from the sheer incredulity of it. "Oh, lady, I am bad news for the family name."

"Precisely why we won't be going into business together." Evangeline stood up, and brushed her dress off, settling it back into place. She walked back around to the table, and settled into her seat across from me, between the Grimsteads.

I turned back to face her, not bothering to hide how thrown I was by this completely ridiculous scenario. "Suit yourself," I replied with an attempt at a glib shrug. "So how'd you dig this bit of family lore up? And you can't tell me that you posted that bounty just to get your long lost sister brought to your doorstep?"

"Absolutely not. Tell me, what do you know of your family?"

"I don't have a family. I was orphaned as a small child and taken in by nuns. I don't remember my parents at all, and I definitely don't remember having siblings. And if it helps, I don't remember having a name before the one they gave me at the convent."

Evangeline tapped her delicate fingers on the table. "Fascinating." She leaned forward. "Our father, Robert Mercer, came out here from England as a young man to act for *his* father back when he was getting the business off the ground.

He met and eventually fell in love with Celeste Cadeaux-Delamer, the daughter of a French merchant family."

"Her reputation was not in good repair," Magnus chimed in. "She was considered a 'wild child', even by her family's standards. They said she took too much interest in unladylike things."

"I can tell which parent I take after already," I said.

"Quite. But since Celeste's father had left France to improve his family's reputations, her behaviour could not continue in such a manner. She needed propriety in her life. At that time, Robert Mercer found himself in the path of Celeste Cadeaux-Delamer at every social event. He noticed her when he had never noticed her before. Of course there is nothing strange about that. Young people notice each other suddenly all the time."

"You say that like it *is* strange," I interrupted. "Do you have a reason to think it was magic or do you just have no idea how attraction between people works?"

He ignored me and continued his story. "Very soon they are in love. Mercer's father did not approve the match, but it's hard to put a stop to things here in the Caribbean when you're all the way in the British Isles. The marriage went ahead. Officially, Celeste's reputation was solidified, things settled down, tongues mostly stopped wagging. The happy couple had a set of twin girls. Almost a year after the daughters were born, Celeste boarded a ship with her children to visit her family who were living on a nearby island. There was a large, unexpected storm during the voyage, and a number of people on board perished, including Celeste and one of her daughters. It was a tragedy. Mercifully, one daughter, Evangeline, survived. Robert Mercer threw himself into his business and raising his surviving daughter to deal with the immense grief. He never recovered from it. He died younger than he ought to have, leaving the shipping business to Evangeline at such a tender age."

"Great story. Change some names, chuck it on the stage, and you could be the new Shakespeare," I said.

"That's our parents," Evangeline snapped.

"*Your* parents," I replied. "To me it's a fairy story you kidnapped me and chained me to a chair to listen to. But Magnus, supposing I believe a single word out of your lying mouth, are you going to tell me what happened *unofficially?*"

"*Unofficially*, Philippe Cadeaux-Delamer, Celeste's father, was accused of being involved with the occult," Magnus said, finally looking interested in the conversation. "There were rumours that Celeste's mother may not have been entirely human."

"Oh, for fuck's sake, people would've notice if she was some weird mythical creature, wouldn't they?" I said. "Oh, there's Mrs Delamer, she's the one with the blue bonnet and the wings."

"Celeste's mother died in childbirth." Magnus smiled at me, if such an expression could be called a smile. It gave me the heebie-jeebies. "At least, that's what they said. If she wasn't entirely human, it's possible she returned to her people."

"I liked it better earlier this evening when I had no living family," I muttered.

Lysander stifled a laugh. He was probably contemplating the virtues of orphanhood too.

"Before my father died," Evangeline interrupted, "he revealed in his last letter to me that Mother had chosen him specifically to bear children with. Their children were the key to unlocking a great magical secret. That's when I found out you weren't dead at all, that Mother had escaped with you. I needed you to find the other half of the key." Her eyes glittered with feverish avarice as she looked at me.

This was getting worse and worse. Violence, I could deal with. Madness, I wasn't prepared for. You never knew what mad people would do next.

"And out of all the people in the world, you just happened to *guess* it was me you were looking for?" My voice was too shrill for my liking.

She waved her hand dismissively. "Oh, Magnus is good at tracking people down. We were afraid you were dead or down in the antipodes, but no, you were still here. Mother unfortunately is dead, according to Magnus' spells and his spells are very good, but once we found out that the notorious Magpie Flint was the missing sister we were searching for..."

"All my troubles started," I finished her sentence. "Look, any chance you can take whatever magical information you need from me and just let me go on my way?"

Evangeline snorted in a most unladylike way. "And let you go about committing crimes all over the Caribbean wearing my face? I don't think so. I'm sorry, sister dearest, it's the gallows for you tomorrow. I grew up an only child, and I'm not used to sharing." She motioned to Magnus. "Let's get what we need."

Magnus Grimstead rose and brought over a small box of what I can only guess were sorcerous tools: bottles of liquids and powders, knives of various sizes. It was leagues above Lysander and his chalk.

Speaking of whom, I cast a desperate glance at Lysander, hoping he could read the question in my eyes. He lifted a blond eyebrow at me before his father sharply called him over.

Guess I could expect no help from that quarter.

The guards on either side of me started to unchain me from the chair as Evangeline personally cleared the table of drinks. I twisted and kicked but I was at a significant disadvantage, still being chained to myself. As one man leaned across me to unlock the shackle on my left arm, I bit his ear, nearly taking it clean off, and causing him to retreat, howling.

"For God's sake, men! She's just one woman. Get her on the table and stop dilly-dallying," Evangeline snapped, apparently unmoved by the plight of her nearly de-eared employee.

"Come in here and help them," I suggested, nearly elbowing another one in the eyesocket. "I'll bite your nose off and then no one will confuse us ever again."

"No thank you," she replied. "I'm educated. I know well enough not to tangle with an enemy in an area of their strength."

That almost felt like a compliment.

Compliment or not, I lost the fight against the four men at arms who succeeded in hauling me onto the table. Now lying on my back, looking up at the dark ceiling, I was still trying to shake off the men at arms.

"We need her to be still."

"I'll take care of it." That was Lysander's voice. A few seconds later, he whispered in my ear. "Listen to me. This is a harmless ritual. It'll be over in a few minutes and you'll be left alone for the night. Just go with what I say."

I didn't have time to analyse anything. Did I trust him? He was Magnus Grimstead's son. But he was his least favourite son.

There were no good options.

A memory of his soft lips flashed unbidden to my mind.

Ugh. Fine. I'd trust him.

I stopped struggling.

"Good," he said and took my arms from the guards, pulling me into a reclining pose, my head and ribcage supported against him. He pulled up my shirt, exposing my stomach.

"Hey, what—no—" I shouted. I tried to move but now I was caught in trap, because there was no way Lysander was stronger than me.

Evangeline sat in her plush armchair, well back from the table, leaning forward curiously as Magnus came forward and began drawing symbols on the flesh of my belly with a sharp tipped metal rod, angry red welts rising where it passed.

"You fucking bastards," I shouted.

"Be patient," Lysander hissed in my ear, barely audible.

Magnus was chanting in a language I didn't know. He drew symbols on my stomach in a deep purple liquid, with a soft brush that tickled me. Then he sprinkled a green powder, then a pungent yellow powder. He drew symbols in the air. It became harder to breathe as the air tightened, or thickened.

"What's he doing?" I asked, stupidly, knowing what the answer was going to be.

"Magic," Lysander replied in my ear, awe and jealousy at war in his voice. "Real, proper magic."

I focused on the familiar smell of Lysander: parchment, exotic flowers, and rare spice. I wished he was still in his linen shirt, not these layers. Still, I could feel his heartbeat at my back, because it was fast and hard. I hoped it was from fear, not excitement.

As the air pressure in the room became oppressively heavy, I tried not to shake at the thought of what would happen to me when it was all let loose. Lysander surreptitiously kissed the back of my head. Maybe he hadn't betrayed me.

And then Magnus Grimstead set my stomach on fire.

31

I screamed.

I think that's a natural reaction to being set on fire.

The pain was blinding. I cursed everyone in the room and their mothers, fathers, all their ancestors and all their progeny.

Then all the pain went away and there was no sign of the fire having ever existed. My stomach was unscarred, un-blistered, and as Magnus brushed away the ash, the only thing that remained from the whole weird ritual was...

A map. Or part of a map. It didn't make a whole lot of sense to me: part nautical directions, part star map, and directions in a language I'd never seen.

From Magnus's gleeful hiss and Evangeline's joyful squeal, this was exactly what they wanted.

They crowded around my stomach with paper to sketch the symbols.I looked up at Lysander.

"Are you hurt?" he whispered, frowning.

"Only briefly," I whispered back.

His face and shoulders relaxed, and he leaned his forehead against mine for a moment.

I was distracted by a shout from my new sister. "It's not complete? Magnus, what do you mean it's not complete? Where would the rest of the information be?"

"Hush." He shot her a look, and gestured at me.

Evangeline glared at me and mastered herself. "Return her," she barked at the men at arms. "Ensure she is watched all night, and that she has no visitors." She narrowed her eyes at Lysander. Clearly, he hadn't been as subtle as he'd hoped.

"Let me know if you need help finding our family treasure," I said to her as they manhandled me past her. "Pirates are famously good at finding treasure. And technically it's half mine."

Evangeline looked at me. "Go fuck yourself," she said in a tone that was so much like mine, it was spooky.

BACK IN MY ROOM SLASH PRISON, WHICH WAS MOODILY LIT WITH two oil lamps, I paced the expensive carpet, unable to settle despite feeling exhausted. I rubbed my stomach under my shirt, which didn't hurt but still tingled in the aftermath of whatever magic Magnus had worked. Or maybe it was all in my head.

Who had hidden that map there? Was it really my mother? Was Evangeline Mercer really my twin sister? It all sounded too preposterous to be true, and yet too preposterous to be lies. Women like Angie didn't invent ties to women like me. The most realistic part of her whole spiel was the part where she wanted me dead so I couldn't go around living my life with 'her' face.

163

I was so lost in my thoughts that I missed the click of the door unlocking, and only heard it open. Carelessness like that would get me killed.

"I'll kill you where you stand!" I spat, managing a half decent swing.

The intruder was well prepared, catching my arm and kicking the door shut behind them. "I'll take my chances," came the even tones of Commodore St Stephen. I dropped my arm. He locked the door behind him, and in the gloom of the large room, I didn't see where he put the key. A pity.

"Miss me?" I asked, more out of habit than interest.

"I heard you were taken away by Miss Mercer, Lysander and Magnus Grimstead. My men reported hearing a lot of commotion, but no specifics." He shifted uncomfortably. "I wanted to see if you were harmed."

"Did you send people to spy?" A smile spread across my face.

He sighed.

"I don't trust either the Grimsteads or Miss Mercer to behave honourably. Least of all where you are concerned." He gazed down at me, his face half in shadow, but the weight in his eyes was inescapable.

I knew that expression. Responsibility. He felt responsible for me. I shivered, and pushed the notion aside. "Well, take a seat, because you're right to be suspicious. The whole thing is way weirder than you could have imagined. It's weirder than *I* could have imagined."

I told Benedict St. Stephen everything that happened in Evangeline's drawing room. I mean, why not? I had every intention of getting out of here alive, but if for some reason I didn't, someone else ought to know that Evangeline was pulling the strings on this whole operation—whatever its end goal was.

The commodore did not disappoint me in his reactions. "Your *sister*," he said, when he could finally talk, saying the word as though it were foreign and he'd never heard it before. "Identical. Twin. Sister."

"It's in the dishonesty. You can really see it in the dishonesty."

"They've been playing me and the entire navy for fools." An anger seeped into his voice that I'd previously only heard directed at me when I was at my most annoying. "Using it as their personal search service. They've put countless lives at risk in this—sorcerous treasure hunt."

"What's making you so mad?" I asked, finally running out of energy for pacing, and sinking onto the floor opposite where he was sitting on the couch. I slumped back against the richly papered wall. "The navy is just the king paying for thugs to look after the English merchants. Is it the magic that offends you? If I had a paper treasure map stuffed down my pants, would this sit better on your conscience?"

"The navy isn't thugs, Flint. We're here to keep order," he snapped. "We're meant to keep people like you *and* Haddrick and Mercer in line. They're not allowed to run roughshod over everyone out there either."

"Well, you probably need to have a chat with them, because," I waved feebly in the direction of the door, "I think Angie has *ambitions*."

"Mmmm." He rubbed his temples. "Which is why you're my favorite of the two sisters."

"I knew you'd warm up to me, commodore. Does that mean you won't let me go to the gallows tomorrow?"

"I will allow justice to be served, Flint." He actually sounded sad when he said that.

I sighed. "Well. Can I have a last request then?"

He eyed me with well deserved suspicion. "That depends."

"You told me you weren't a virgin. I find that really hard to believe. You can't let me go to my grave without telling me how someone got you into bed."

"You wha—" He sputtered. I couldn't see well enough in the low light but I'd wager he was turning red. "That's your last request? It's possibly your last night on earth, and you want to talk about my sex life?"

"Well, what else are we going to talk about?" I shrugged. "Neither of us know anything about sorcery, you're not going to help me plot an escape, and I don't feel like trying to convince you that you're working for a tyrannical system. So that leaves sex."

"At least I can be assured that whatever they did to you, your personality is intact." He seemed to be speaking to himself. He stood and for a moment I thought he was going to walk out the door, but realised he was heading to the cabinet against the far wall. Opening the polished wood doors, he drew out a large green bottle with a cork sealed with wax and red ribbon and two ornate goblets, he turned to me. "Drink?"

"Those weren't there this afternoon."

"They weren't." He worked the cork out with the strength of his grip. "I put them there earlier for you to find, so you could at least have a nice final night."

I pulled myself to standing, and sauntered over to take one of the filled glasses. It was madeira, imported from

Europe. Not my drink of choice, but I'd take it. The liquid was dark in my goblet, and had a rich texture that didn't burn like rum did. It was sweet, but not cloying. It went down easy.

Standing this close to him, I could see stubble had come in across his jaw. I resisted the urge to run my hand over it. "I think I'm a bad influence on you." I licked the beads of red liquid from my lips.

"You've never spoken truer words, Miss Flint." He settled back on the chaise. I went back to my spot on the wall opposite him, but stayed standing this time. "I'm afraid the story of my seduction isn't nearly as interesting as you hope. It is very boring, and I suspect you will laugh."

"Listen, earlier tonight someone told me they had a 'prosaic' story for me then spat out a tale about being my twin and some kind of wild magical heritage. So if your story is even half as boring as that was prosaic…"

He smiled, looking pained. Several minutes passed in silence. I sipped my drink, growing uncomfortable.

"You don't have to—" I started, just as he knocked his entire drink back.

"I come from a good family. My father is nobility of small distinction, and I'm his third son, so I was bound for the military. First sons get the title and the land, second sons go to the church and the third goes to the military. I chose the navy because I loved the sea. I was young when I left home to take up this career, too young to have gotten married and because I was raised to be more honourable than many young men of my station, I never carried on with the servant girls or the baker's daughter or whoever else."

"A stickler for honour from birth."

"Indeed," he said with a ghost of a smile. "I always knew

that seafaring would either be an early grave or a career, so marrying a woman who would either be made a widow or hardly ever see me never seemed right. Besides which, there was no need for marriage. My eldest brother was carrying on the family line admirably, and what was the use of marrying for affection if I was an unreliable husband? She would either be lonely or would stray. One or both of us would be hurt. I could be nothing but a disappointment."

"So far, you're right. It is disappointingly scrupulous. There are priests with less pristine records than you," I told him. "Then what? You met an irresistible woman? A hushed liaison? A secret engagement?"

"I am only seduced by justice," he said gravely, and I stared at him. He laughed, a small huff of air and a broad smile I had only seen once or twice.

"Neptune's balls, I believed you for a second!" I kicked him in the shins as I went over to refill both our goblets. He didn't react to my violence. "Where've you been hiding that sense of humour all this time?"

"I keep it on land. I find it interferes with my duty on the sea. Miss Flint, I wasn't seduced. When you're the captain, you need to keep the respect of your crew. You know that."

I nodded. That was the same in both a pirate and navy vessel.

"When we'd make berth at port towns and go ashore, we'd go to the establishments for sailors who wanted a certain kind of company. The kind of establishment your friend Val runs."

"Right," I said, nodding. "And?"

"And what?" he snapped. "You know how these places work. You pay your money, and you buy the company of a professional. At first I did it because it would seem strange to my crew if I didn't, but—well. I'm human."

"Are you serious?" I exclaimed. "You've only knocked boots with ladies of the night?"

"I treated them with respect and—"

"Commodore, I know you did, and I'm sure you'd keel-haul any member of your crew that behaved poorly toward a professional—or anyone. I'm just surprised that you've never taken a tumble with anyone who propositioned you."

"I *told* you, it wouldn't have been responsible to make offers like that."

"I didn't mean marriage. I meant a fuck."

"I would never compromise a lady's reputation like that."

"Neptune's balls, commodore! There's a world between women of negotiable affection and marriage."

"Not for me there isn't. It would have been too complicated."

"Good news." I drank deeply from my goblet, set it down on the table next to the bottle, and walked towards him. "I'm not a lady, my reputation cannot possibly be more compromised, I'm the simplest woman in the world and I still want to get into those navy-issue trousers of yours."

The commodore looked up at me from where he was seated, then slowly rose to his full height. He reached past me to put his drink down, stepping excitingly close into my personal space without touching. His proximity sent shivers down my spine.

"I still don't understand why," he said softly, his body only inches from mine, close enough that I could feel the heat, even through his clothes, even through mine. "Is it just obstinate contrariness?"

"At first," I admitted. "Then because you were such a

puzzle. You always surprise me. You're dangerous. You're attractive. You look delicious when unshaven. All those good things. But now... I think everyone should know what it's like to fuck someone who wants to fuck them, don't you?"

"I can't save you," he said. "Tomorrow. It's out of my hands. You've already pushed me past my limits."

"I know you can't save me. I'm not asking you to."

"I shot a navy man because I thought he killed you." His voice shook with the confession. I couldn't tell if it was anger or fear. I also didn't know entirely what he was talking about.

"You shot—who?"

"When he shot you and you fell in the ocean."

My mind flashed back to the robbery of the navy ship. I remembered Smith told me that Lieutenant Hatsford, who shot me, was killed but no one knew who took the shot.

"That was you?" Disbelief was clear in my voice. "You were supposed to be below so you didn't have to see us do anything against your principles."

"He was cowardly," St Stephen practically growled. The venom in his voice was unlike anything I had heard before, even when he talked about his disdain for pirates. "Everything was done as negotiated, and he took a coward's shot at you. I thought you were *dead*."

The commodore hesitantly put one hand on my arm and one on the side of my face. I stared up at him, at those eyes that looked so calm and unperturbed most of the time, only to reveal the drowning maelstrom underneath when we were alone.

"I thought you were dead," he repeated.

"I'm here." I ran one hand along his stubbled jawline, brushing my thumb along the prominent cheekbone. "For tonight at least, we're here, we're alive. We've got now."

I stepped in slightly closer, pressing against him. I tilted my face up, only inches away from his lips.

"It's up to you, commodore," I said. "I might be the Caribbean's most wanted, but right now, you're my most wanted. What do you say? Want to be my last request?"

I barely finished talking before his lips caught mine in a crushing kiss.

32

Exhilaration flowed through me as the commodore's mouth explored mine. His lips were sweet from the madeira, and soft, and so bruisingly urgent. I met them with equal fervour, nipping gently at his lip, then soothing the pain with a brush of my tongue.

The commodore groaned and pulled me closer, like he was drowning and I was the only thing keeping him afloat. The heat and hardness of his body made my abdomen tighten in anticipation.

St Stephen broke the kiss first. "You're sure you want this? With me? I can't offer you anything."

"Yes," I said, and grabbed the front of his coat. "Now take your fucking clothes off."

My heart pounded as he threw off his jacket and pulled off his boots. If anyone interrupted this, I'd murder them so hard they'd never know what hit them and they'd be stuck haunting this dismal mansion for eternity.

When he reached for the buttons of his waistcoat, I pushed him back onto the chaise, and sat astride him. "Let me," I said, undoing the buttons of his uniform waistcoat, and pushing it off his shoulders. I pulled the crisp shirt over his head.

I'd fantasized about a moment like this.

Shirtless, with candlelight flickering off his bare flesh, he looked perfect.

He looked at me uncertainly, as though he expected a rebuke or a joke, but I kissed him again as I ran my hands over his chest.

"No tattoos?" I whispered against his mouth. "Or are they somewhere more fun?"

"No tattoos," he replied. He spoke quickly, uninterested in talking now. "Never thought the risk of infection was worth it."

His tongue was finally brave enough to reply to my own and as he thoroughly explored my mouth, my whole body broke out in tingles. Distracted, I barely noticed he too reached the end of his patience with my clothes, deftly ridding me of my waistcoat and my shirt.

My breasts were once again exposed, but this time the commodore drank in the sight of them like he was a man dying of thirst and they were the only water for miles.

"May I-"

"Yes," I cut him off, arching my back, to press them closer to him. He took one in each hand, and kneaded them gently, watching with fascination as goosebumps spread across the tender flesh and the pink nipples tightened to a point immediately. I stifled a cry, and it came out as a moan. He looked up at me, startled, then grinned, a sly smile of male pride.

"Keep going," I told him, rocking my hips against him. "Lick them. It feels good."

He didn't need telling twice. His lips, breath and tongue

filled me with electric sensations that shot straight to my core. I steadied myself on his broad shoulders, his flesh hot to the touch. His breath was coming fast as he worked at my breasts. My head swam with comfortable pleasure, physical and emotional. The look on his face when I had made that noise stayed with me: had the women he'd seen before not reacted? Or was this different for him because he knew I'd never lie for his ego?

This was the first time it wasn't transactional for him, I reminded myself. And I wanted to show him what I wanted to do for him. How much I wanted to do things to him.

"Come on." I kissed him on the chest then turned him toward the bed with a playful shove. "I'd carry you to the bed but we both know that's not going to end with either of us getting any action."

Benedict St Stephen laughed, a low sound that made the walls of my cave of wonders clench. I just about pushed him on the bed and climbed on top of him.

"Aren't I supposed to be the one on top?" he asked, sounding genuinely bemused. My hands on either side of his wide, naked torso, I leaned down to kiss him. His stubble was a rough grain against my face. When my nipples brushed against his chest, his whole body shuddered and he moaned against my mouth.

"Maybe later," I whispered into his neck, breathing feather-light kisses there, until I reached the point where it became shoulder and I nipped him. He groaned. "Tell me to stop if I do anything you don't like."

I explored my way down his chest with kisses, nips and roaming fingers. Every groan and gasp made me wetter, knowing he was finally trusting me with something he had never trusted anyone with me before.

Reaching his breeches, I ran my hand over the large, hard lump and he nearly bucked off the bed.

"Easy, sailor." I grinned. "Save that for when you're inside me." He made a gasping noise I think was laughter. I frowned at the navy breeches. I'd never had to undo one of these.

"How do I undo these?"

"For heaven's sake, woman!" With reflexes like a snake, the commodore sat up, undid the offending trousers and flung them off. If he was wearing anything under it, it was gone in the same motion. He toppled me onto my back, and swiftly dispensed with the remainder of my clothes too.

He looked down at me, like a man dying of thirst.

"I want to touch," he ground out in a voice that had no veneer of civility, but was all base desire.

"Touch me, sailor."

His hands and his lips were all over my body. Instinctively, I opened my legs and wrapped them around his waist, his cock pressing against my seam. It was pulsing and hot. My core was doing its best to simply pull it in through sheer power of horniness, but I clenched and told it to shut up. Not yet. Not yet.

As a pirate, the commodore was always a part of my world. As Magpie, he'd been a big part of my world for the last little while. And right now, he was my whole world. Nothing existed except for his hands, his mouth, the weight of his body. The sounds of his pleasure made me grin, in between my own gasps.

One his hands made its way between legs, moving his cock aside and sinking into the softness of my womanhood. I stifled a cry and he froze, pulling it out.

"I'm sorry, was I not..."

"No, you're definitely supposed to. That's where I keep the good stuff. Soon to include your cock."

He shut his eyes and made a sputtering noise that may have been a suppressed laugh.

"Are you taking this seriously?" The question wasn't annoyed, there was laughter in his eyes alongside the burning lust.

"Aye," I said. I reached down to stroke his cock. His eyelids fluttered shut and his mouth formed an 'o' of pleasure. "Have to remember who you have in bed, is all."

"I could never forget," he managed to say.

"And I'm very serious about showing how much I want you."

I gently rolled him onto his back, and sat astride him, stroking the soft flesh of his cock. If anyone asks I'll tell them it was massive and it's lucky our ship didn't sink, but truly, while was a respectable member of its ranks, it was only above average in stature and not one for Val's record books. It didn't matter, only the man attached mattered.

And I didn't think he was going to hold out much longer if I teased him like this.

I scooted forward and with my eyes locked on his, I lowered myself slowly onto his shaft, both of us breathing hard as inch by inch it slid into the hot, tight embrace of my womanhood.

I placed his fingers on that magical sweet spot just above the entrance, his calloused fingertips moving over it and sending delicious tingles to my stretched core.

"Keep them there," I told him. "And we'll come undone."

I leaned forward and he began to thrust, my body fighting the loss of him every time, then welcoming him back with a pleasurable stretch that fanned the flames of an orgasm building in my core. We were wrapped up in each other and the growing pleasure from not just from his cock or his fingers, but also the way he looked at me. He looked at me like I was a wonder and a joy. He whispered my name between his groans, until the he became insensible, and he became blind with pleasure. His orgasm hit him savagely, tearing any composure he had left apart. The sight of his wildness sent me tumbling over the edge, losing all sense of anything except being thrown apart and pleasure lighting up every nerve in my body.

When I could think and see again, I was lying on the commodore's chest, both of us breathing hard and sweaty.

"What did you think?" I asked, hoping he didn't regret his decision.

"I think..." His chest rose beneath me as he took a long, shuddering breath. "I think I wasted a lot of time on that ship."

33

The trial was boring. A lot of people in black robes and even stupider wigs than usual made speeches about what a menace to society I was. I tried to explain my side, but I realised quickly that would just make things go on even longer. There was a lot of procedure, and it didn't help that they were all drinking and didn't even have the decency to give me any. So much for "polite society."

Evangeline smirked at me the whole trial, and the commodore avoided my eyes. In fact, I'd never seen him less enthused about law and order. I couldn't bring myself to be mad at him, not after he floated the idea that I should be sent to a religious institution for reform—an idea that was promptly shouted down. As an alternative to death, it was sort of sweet.

After the sham of a trial, I was (to the surprise of no one) found guilty and sentenced to hang by the neck until dead. A waste of everyone's time–if they'd just asked, I'd have told them I was guilty at the start.

They were supposed to transport me straight to the jailhouse at the fort, right next to the gallows, but just as the trial wrapped up, a very beleaguered messenger made an appearance. There was a lot of whispering. Evangeline was called over and there was even more whispering.

I couldn't eavesdrop because every time I tried to shuffle closer, the man assigned to guard me, who was the same size and build as Haddrick—perhaps another lost identical twin? —would yank my chains so hard I tumbled to the floor.

Eventually the judge announced that an enormous herd of semi-feral goats had infested the land around the gallows and the jailers were locked inside their own facility. Considerable damage had been done to the prison transport wagon so it was unable to fetch me. Evangeline gave me suspicious looks, but my obvious surprise and obscenely loud laughter reassured her that I had not somehow orchestrated this while being locked in her house, even if she didn't know that I'd been occupied bedding the commodore.

So that's how I came to be locked up again in my sister's worst guest bedroom, while some poor souls deal with the feral goat problem.

Naturally, that meant I was going to try to escape.

I didn't have to think too hard about it. As I was leaning out the window measuring the drop to the ground, trying to figure out if I could make a rope out of the drapery (and if I could then somehow escape without the servants in the courtyard noticing me—I didn't fancy my odds) a familiar red parrot sailed across the sky, grasping a small package in its claws.

I let him in and shut the window. "Dauntless, you magnificent bastard, am I glad to see you."

He flapped his wings in acknowledgment. It seemed he understood that his ear-piercing squawks would be a threat to both our lives in this situation. He was always the better one out of the two of us at knowing when to shut his mouth. He pecked at the package he'd dropped.

Inside it, I found a new set of lockpicks, a map of each of the levels of the house and a note from Val.

Dearest M,

Sorry about last night. We tried to rescue you, figuring you'd be less guarded while everyone was at the party, but we never guessed they'd take you as the guest of honour. We did get a decent look about the place so you have some maps. We robbed Magnus Grimstead's study of a lot of books. From chatting to the servants, we also learned that there's no real guard roster apart from having two people on your door at all times. They're over-confident. We've delayed your transport to the jail so you have a little time to escape. We've got a contact at Pier 32 who'll let you take their dinghy out of the bay and meet us around the head-land. Good luck.

Val

I stuffed the note in my boots and studied the maps until I was fairly certain I could follow them without looking. I looked at Dauntless. "You memorised these?"

I didn't know a parrot could toss its head arrogantly, but clearly Dauntless could do things with a parrot body that pushed the boundaries of avian biology.

"Right. I have a knife. I'm going to pick the lock, then wait for them to come and investigate. You go for the eyes on the first; I'll stab the next guy and finish the first guy. Okay?"

The parrot opened its beak, then clapped it shut. There was a long silence before it nodded.

"You're so much less argumentative in this form. It makes teamwork much easier," I told him, grabbing the lockpicks.

Dauntless cuffed me over the head with his large wing as he took flight.

I've never been so happy to bicker with an ex.

Val had sent a good set of picks. Picking a lock without having to twist myself back to front like I'd done at the party was much easier. Within a minute, the lock made a satisfying click. With Dauntless in position on top of the bed's canopy, I pulled open one of the double doors, staying out of sight behind it.

"What the hell?" came the voice of a guard. "Did you leave this unlocked?"

"No," his buddy replied. The first man came inside, clearing the doorway.

"She's gone—argh!" Dauntless swooped down and raked his face with his...talons? Pointy parrot feet. Look, I'm no parrot expert. The important thing is, the commotion drew the second man inside. I slit his throat from behind before he knew what was happening and did the same to his parrot-maimed friend a few seconds later.

"Good job," I told Dauntless, wiping the knife I'd palmed off Wilfred Haddrick on the shirt of one of the recently deceased. "Let's get out of here. I got more blood on me than I planned."

Dauntless eyed me beadily, then flew off into the corridor. I hurried after him, closing the door behind me. From the outside, it looked peaceful. It might be some time before they discovered the carnage within.

We made our way across the third floor without running into anyone, and took a set of side stairs down to the second floor. We waited without breathing (or flapping) while a trio of matching men-at-arms walked past the door, watching through the keyhole as they disappeared into a side room.

"I don't know if we'll be able to get out of the house without being noticed looking like this. Might need some different clothes," I whispered to Dauntless. He bit my shoulder, then shook his head. "Fine. We'll go for speed."

We slipped into the corridor and hurried down its length, taking a sharp turn from the servants' corridor, and through a door that opened out in the main hall. The lights were brighter here, and the floor was carpeted. Just as the main staircase downstairs came into view, I stopped dead in my tracks. Voices were coming up the stairs.

"It's Magnus Grimstead. And someone else." I looked around at the doors on either side of me. Which of these rooms was empty? Dauntless flapped his wings urgently. Shit. I would have to pick one at random and hope.

"Captain Flint! Over here!" I whirled around at the sound of my name.

Georgiana Weatherby, the governor's daughter, was waving me over from a doorway. I didn't waste a moment.

"Thanks kid," I told her once Dauntless and I were safely inside the room. "You saved my life."

"It's my pleasure. I'm glad you're escaping." She curtsied elegantly and unnecessarily. "Is that your parrot?"

"This is Captain Dauntless. He's an ex. He's normally a human but he's under a curse," I answered distractedly while I looked around the room. It was definitely a woman's dressing room, but it didn't at all match Georgiana Weatherby. "We're trying to uncurse him but the Grimsteads aren't very chatty about any topic that isn't Magnus's plan for total naval dominion. Hey, kid, whose room is this?"

"Evangeline Mercer's," she replied promptly. "She was

called to an emergency at the town on the other side of the island, so I'm snooping."

"I like your instincts." I opened a drawer at random. It was filled with pins.

"Since you're here and you need to get out without being recognised," Georgiana hesitated. "What if you wear Evangeline's dress and wig? Since you're identical twins and all."

Dauntless let out a squawk, and beat his wings in agitation.

"I'll explain later," I told him. I turned back to Georgiana. "How'd you know that?"

"I eavesdropped," she said with a wide-eyed, earnest look. "They put guards on the doors, but they didn't think about how much you can hear through the wall if you're listening from the next room."

"Kid, you were born to be a criminal." I looked at Angie's wig sitting on its stand and exchanged a look with the parrot. "All right, let's do it."

Noble ladies' clothes are an absolute pain in the ass to put on. That's why they have a minimum of five servants each to help them. Luckily Georgiana knew what to do, helping me with the under layers, stays and all that nonsense. I refused to give up my footwear, arguing that the skirts were so long no one would notice my boots. I also negotiated her down from the full set of layers to something more practical. Georgiana insisted it was in fact all practical, but I refused to believe her. What could you possibly need all these underskirts for, unless you were smuggling something? Anyway, I just needed to look enough like Evangeline to get out of the house and down to the docks. If anyone stopped to count my underskirts, they wouldn't live to tell the tale.

"I'm going to think twice before picking a fight with a lady of quality," I grunted, as Georgiana deftly pinned a stomacher into place on the dress, "knowing just how many pins they're all wearing. Do they realise how dangerous they could be if they put their minds to it? Look at this skirt, Dauntless. I could hide a powder keg under here and no one would know."

Dauntless squawked bleakly.

"What do you think?" Georgiana asked, once the wig was pinned on. She turned me towards the mirror.

I stared at the glass. My mass of hair was tamed and tucked away underneath the wig, and my face smeared with whatever cosmetic concoction ladies use to make it look like they've never seen the outdoors.

Georgiana said what I was thinking. "I think it's... spooky."

"Fuck me, we really are twins," I breathed, as Evangeline Mercer looked back at me from the mirror. There was no doubt about it now that I was in her clothes. My stomach roiled at the sight, this undeniable proof of our connection, but I pushed it aside. My life depended on this. I could be disgusted at my relatives later.

"Right, let's get out of here."

Georgiana shoved a parasol into my hand. "Can't let the sun touch you. Now we go take some air."

"Imagine the horror, getting a tan in the Caribbean." I followed her out of the dressing room.

As we descended the stairs, we encountered a small crowd in the foyer. A well dressed servant turned, surprise clear on his face. "Ah, Miss Mercer. I did not realise you had returned. You have some callers who wish to see you."

34

I stared at the servant, my mind completely blank. One of my rare moments of speechlessness had struck. As I locked eyes silently with the man, he coughed uncomfortably into a gloved hand, eyes flicking between me and Georgiana.

"Forgive me, Miss Mercer, I wasn't aware you and Miss Weatherby were about to take the air—"

"I'm sure Miss Mercer can defer her constitutional for a spot of tea," came a shrill voice from the crowd. I glanced at Georgiana with what I hoped was well disguised panic.

"I would be pleased to take some tea before our walk, Miss Mercer," Georgiana said, only a slight widening in her eyes betraying anxiety. They trained posh ladies to be world class liars, I was impressed.

But I was a world class criminal. I was equal to the task.

I raised my chin, and tried to pitch my voice in the cool, cultured tones of Evangeline Mercer, and not let on that this frightened me more than boarding a navy ship. "I'd be delighted. Prepare the tea."

With Georgiana's subtle help I ended up in the correct

'sitting room', and seated in the correct chair. The guests consisted of the old woman with no chin who'd been unnecessarily mean to me last night, her husband, two younger ladies, Wilfred Haddrick, and a woman he introduced as his younger cousin, Catherine. His cousin shared his height and looked like she'd be able to break any unwanted suitors over her knee, a quality I always liked in a woman.

"I hope you all enjoyed the festivities last night," I said, trying to mimic the small half smile I'd seen Angie do. "Nobody was too frightened, I hope?"

"Miss Mercer, I told you last night, I was most unimpressed," the old woman started.

"I thought it was thrilling," Georgiana jumped in.

Wilfred grunted. "It was just one pirate, we had it under control."

I wasn't required to say anything else as the discussion raged on. To my pleasant surprise, Miss Haddrick was a damn sight smarter than her brother. I gathered a lot of useful gossip about prominent residents in Port Elizabeth and certain merchant and naval captains. Throw in some coarse language, a fist fight, some bad smells and it wouldn't have been much different from listening to sailors chatter in a tavern. It was almost a shame when the tea arrived.

Cups were set in front of all the guests, and the teapot placed near me. Georgiana signalled at me frantically with her eyes.

Silence as everyone looked at me.

"Miss Mercer?" Georgiana gestured at the teapot.

"Miss Mercer, do serve the tea before it chills," Mrs No-Chin commanded.

I'm a pirate and even I could tell she was being rude. "We're in the Caribbean. If there is one thing we are safe from, it's chills." I managed to stop the retort in its tracks by saying the words through clenched teeth. Fortunately, it sounded like Angie being cutting, so no one noticed anything was amiss.

"That is uncalled for, Mrs Comerford," Miss Haddrick replied coolly enough to be a danger to the tea's temperature. "We all know Miss Mercer is an impeccable hostess with the finest manners. I'll ask you kindly not to slight my future sister-in-law in such a manner."

Then she looked at me with a challenge in her eyes.

Thankfully, at that moment, an avian shriek rent the air. Dauntless hurtled into the room, raking his claws over the tops of everyone's heads. As the party ducked, he sent the china on the table flying. With a second shriek, he vanished out the door.

"Georgiana!" I scolded. "Your pet! I told you that you must contain him!"

"I beg your pardon, Miss Mercer, everyone. I don't know how he got out of his cage!" Georgiana did not miss her cue.

"Excuse us a moment. We will secure the bird, and order a fresh tea service." I grabbed Georgiana by the arm. Before any of the guests recovered their senses or processed what had happened, we hustled from the room, rushing for the front door.

AFTER THE GLOOM OF THE HOUSE, THE SUNLIGHT BLINDED ME. I blinked to adjust to it. It was almost as bad as coming up on deck after being in the hold, except without the benefit of an eyepatch.

Dauntless sailed out the door after us and I slammed it shut. "Right, let's head down to the docks."

Georgina didn't reply, only pointed. Her face was a mask of fear.

At the far end of the property, a carriage pulled into a carriage house.

"Miss Mercer is back. Much sooner than she's expected." Georgiana turned to me in fear. "She's going to realise what you've done."

"Delay her as much as possible. Play dumb, pretend you had no idea it wasn't her in the tea room. Protect yourself at all costs, all right? Here." I pressed the lockpicks into her hand. "Practice with these. I think you'll find them handy. Good luck, kid. Come on, Dauntless."

I got out of there like there was a bee in my bonnet.

35

The rest of the escape was mostly uneventful. As I walked through the well-to-do part of town, everyone steered well clear of me. That told me everything I needed to know about how friendly and approachable my twin was. People threw me curious glances. No doubt wondering why I was alone, or why I didn't have a parasol or why I was wearing the wrong gloves or some other social faux pas. It cheered me up that Angie would have to find some way to explain all that later without outright saying it had been a filthy pirate masquerading as her. If Dauntless hadn't been there, I probably would've gotten distracted, getting up to no good as "Angie." Good thing he was there to keep me firmly focussed getting out of dodge.

Once I got to the part of town where my fancy wig and dress stuck out like a sore thumb, I ducked into an alley, and shucked off the fancy outer layers. I threw a slightly damp dress grabbed from a washing line over the top of the complicated underlayers. Whispering an apology to the woman whose dress I stole, I left Angie's expensive wig as recompense. Hopefully some of the jewels in that thing were worth something. Angie's dress itself, I bundled up and tucked under my arm. Val would fucking love it.

Now far less noticeable, I ran through the streets, with Dauntless flying above me and keeping an eye out for trouble. When we got to the entrance to the dock, he squawked loudly. I ducked behind a low wall and peered over.

Navy. Lots of navy.

Damn. Either they knew I escaped or they suspected I might.

I felt a stab of bitter pain in my chest. It was unreasonable. I knew that the commodore would have to do his job, regardless of what happened between us personally. Regardless of what happened last night. Even though he tried for leniency today at the trial.

I was jolted from my thoughts by Dauntless squawking and scratching out the letters FOLO in the dirt. Then he took flight.

We went through alleys and side streets, emerging before a channel that he indicated I should jump into. It wasn't the cleanest but I've swum in the filthy waters of Boneyard Bay, and my other option was the gallows. I dived in, letting the current carry me out toward the port. The channel spat me out near a length of piers. Hauling myself up, I came unexpectedly face to face with a navy man who looked oddly familiar.

He looked me up and down. "Magpie Flint."

"Me? No. I get that all the time, so you're not the first fellow to make the mistake." I laughed, and my hand inched towards my knife.

"I heard you might come this way. You saved my life

once," he said quietly. Well, that wasn't what I expected. My hand paused, and I squinted at the lad.

"You're from when we stole all the navy clothes." I suddenly remembered the man didn't want to undress.

"Yes," he replied. "You have some good friends, Flint. Brave friends. I understand why, I think, if you treat your friends even twice as well as you treat your enemies."

He checked his pocket watch. "It seems pretty quiet. I guess it's about time for me to do a patrol. Pier 32 is right behind you," he said.

"Lad." I caught his arm as he started to stroll past, carefully not looking at me. "Thanks. I owe you."

"No. You've already saved my life. Now I save yours. We're square."

Dauntless squawked impatiently. I didn't wait for the navy man to change his mind. I jumped into the small boat, and started putting as much ocean between me and Port Elizabeth as I could.

THE SEA WAS ON FIRE AND THE SKY WAS BEING SWALLOWED BY darkness when I finally reached *The Queen's Liberty*. The crew's cheering was deafening. Val hugged me first when I clambered onboard, her familiar embrace tight and fierce. I hugged her back with equal fervour.

"I thought we lost you when we botched it yesterday. I am so glad to see you alive." She sobbed unashamedly into my chest.

"I'm fine, I'm fine. I'm fucking hard to kill, you know that," I told her, hiding my own tears in her shoulder. "I'm just glad we saved you."

"Welcome back, captain." Sebastian's soft voice gently interrupted our reunion. "Is there anything we need to stay for or shall we make sail?"

"Make sail—shit. Wait." I paused. The trio of Haddrick, Mercer and Grimstead were all evil and insane. They needed to be stopped. "We need to plan. Take us towards that island we passed and anchor around the west side, out of sight of the main shipping lines. Fly Haddrick and Mercer colours."

"Captain, what's yer thinking?" Smith asked.

"We need to talk, I have a lot of new information. Magnus Grimstead and Evangeline Mercer are after a magical treasure that they think will give them...some kind of supernatural advantage. Their goal is total dominion over the seas."

I wasn't ready to tell everyone about my connection with Evangeline just yet.

"We stole a lot of books from Magnus's library," Val said. "Judith is looking over them now in the hope that we can reverse the curse on Dauntless and recreate some of Lysander's magic. The crew told me what he was capable of."

I winced. Yeah, now we didn't have the special cannon protection or the ability to call wind at will, and the enemy did. "Here's hoping Judith is a real quick study."

"Hear fucking hear," came Dauntless's voice.

The sun had finished its descent while we were talking, and the human Captain Dauntless came out of the darkness. As a human, Edward Dauntless was more than six foot three, broad shouldered, and had sculpted features that I was pretty sure he'd somehow stolen off a fancy Italian statue. His dark curly hair normally cascaded over his shoulders but at the moment he had it tied back. It only served to accentuate his precisely trimmed goatee. How had he found the time to do that when he was a parrot half the time? I was a full time human and I barely found time to brush my hair.

Val stamped on my foot discretely. "Stop swooning," she hissed.

"I'm not swooning, I'm very tired," I hissed back. "I didn't get enough sleep last night."

"Those bastards," Val muttered, shaking her head. She caught the guilty look on my face. "Wait—*no*. We've been worried sick about you and you've been—*who, Maggie?*"

"Shhh, not here," I whispered. "I'll tell you later."

"You'll tell me now."

"Fine. It was the commodore."

"Then why the fuck didn't *he* rescue you?"

"You know." I gesticulated vaguely. "Morals?"

I've never seen Val so unimpressed. "For fucks' sake Maggie. Next time you're going to fuck someone while being held captive, can you fuck someone who's going to set you free? Lysander would've done it."

I made a face. She was probably right.

Ignoring Val's disappointed glare, I called a meeting in my cabin of my trusted advisors and stumbled inside.

The first thing I noticed inside was that someone had cleaned up. My cabin had started to stink with a rotating cast of five of us living there, and I wasn't the tidiest person in the first place. Now all the glassware was clean, the liquor was refilled, the bed had clean linen, the floor was mopped and all my clothes were hung up. I think they were even *washed*.

I looked at Val.

"I wanted to get it nice for you for when we rescued you," she said, twisting her fingers together. "Kept me optimistic."

"Thanks." I looked down at the soggy mess of clothes I was wearing. "Sorry about this."

She waved her hand dismissively. "I'm used to it in my line of work. As soon as I clean one mess, someone makes another."

"At least I brought you a present?" I finally remembered the dress I'd been clutching under my arm like my life depended on it. Val's little gasp of joy made me immediately glad I hung onto it. My best friend deserved nice things more than my evil twin sister did.

We sat at the large table. Once everyone had arrived and been served a drink, I laid out what had happened since I got taken from the chapel of Santa Lucia all the way to when I rowed up alongside the ship. I only left out the bit with the commodore last night. That was private to me, the commodore and now Val.

Naturally, everyone was appropriately and dramatically surprised at the revelation about Evangeline.

"Ye really look just like her?" Smith's pipe fell from his lips into his drink. He fished out the pipe and drained his glass, tobacco ash and all.

"Everyone bought the disguise today," I replied. "Even Wilfred Haddrick, though we all know he's all brawn. His cousin looked like she might've got the largest share of the family brain."

"Can we see the map on your stomach?" Judith asked eagerly.

"Tomorrow," I said, tiredness crashing down on me. "I'm wearing a lot of layers now and a posh lady's corset. It'll take an age to get undressed. Tomorrow everyone can ogle the magic map on my stomach."

"Do you think they'll stop chasing you now?" Val asked, ever practical.

"No. Evangeline wants me off the seas. It's personal for her." I stared into my drink for a few long seconds, before looking back up at my assembled friends. "Plus she said the map isn't complete, so she needs me or at least my body to find the rest."

After they ran out of questions, Val filled me in on what had happened from their end. As soon as she was reunited with the crew, she took a group and hid out in the city. By asking around, they soon found out about the party and decided to break me out then. Of course it all went wrong, but with the books stolen from Magnus Grimstead's study, Judith had cobbled together a spell that summoned all the wild goats on the island to the gallows. The effect was even more overwhelming than they'd hoped. The destroyed prisoner wagon was a bonus from a fire that got out of control. As a result, my execution had been successfully delayed, allowing them to send Dauntless for the second breakout attempt.

"Well done." I was genuinely impressed. "Nice work, Judith. So, who took Evangeline out of the house with an urgent message?"

"That wasn't us. That might have just been genuine luck." Val looked closely at me and stood up. "Good chat, captain, but I think you need some rest now so you're fresh to lead us in the morning."

"Aye." I lifted my glass to her. "Thanks, all of you. You're a mighty loyal crew, the best any reprobate captain could ask for."

The departing crew members made their well wishes until only Dauntless remained. He stood by the door, eyes fixed on mine.

"Do you want me to stay or go?" His eyes burned like he knew the answer already.

"Stay," I said.

He slammed the door shut.

36

———

Dauntless crossed the room in two strides. Before I could protest or resist, he lifted me out of my chair, and pulled me into a kiss.

I buried myself in his mouth and the feeling of home that washed over me, lost in the taste of sea, sweat and rum. I was startled when his hard body pulled away from me.

"You *scared* me, Maggie," he said, his voice husky, one hand still around my waist, the other cradling my face. "I thought we might really lose you this time."

I opened my mouth to say something flippant, something brave, but the words caught in my throat. The rawness in Dauntless's voice and the emotion in his eyes completely shattered my defences. All the bravado I'd been hiding behind since I left the ship to deliver the commodore and Lysander shattered to a thousand pieces.

"I was terrified," I admitted, shutting my eyes, tears pooling on my lashes. "These people were so unpredictable, so cruel. I had no idea from one minute to the next what they were going to do. The commodore, at least I could rely on to...

follow the law, I guess, but everyone else... For all I knew they were going to drag me out at midnight and sacrifice me to some god Magnus met in a dream."

I took a deep breath that sounded like a juddering sob and buried my face in my hands. I was trembling all over, the aftermath of all that fear. A human reaction, I knew, but I hated reminders that I was human.

Dauntless kissed the top of my head with a gentleness I forgot he had—I had made myself forget he had because it was easier to remember him as a braggadocious asshole—and sat me down.

"Let's get you into something dry." He hunted around the cabin. "I care about you, Maggie, but you're damp and whatever you swam in smells terrible, and I finally found some decent clothes to wear."

An incredibly elegant snort-hiccup escaped me.

"Right. Stand up. Chin up. Arms up."

I numbly followed his instructions as he began to strip the damp layers off of me. "I can undress myself you know," I grumbled, as he untied a petticoat and it pooled at my feet.

"Yes, but I'm so much better at it," he replied with a toothy grin.

I laughed and felt better.

"Neptune's briny beard, how many petticoats are you wearing?" he asked as he got to the third one.

"It's a disguise."

"And who was going to check your petticoats? Haddrick? Surely you were going to shoot him before he got his thick head under your skirts."

"Stop worrying about the petticoats and get me out of this corset," I told him. I was down to the last petticoat and I didn't have anything on underneath. I wasn't worried about modesty; he'd seen my feminine cave of wonders too many times to count. It was just that I hadn't quite decided how I wanted this to go yet.

Was I just going to put on the pants he'd placed slightly out of my reach on the table and then we'd get drunk, or...

"That's a really nice corset," he said. "You keeping it?"

"Hell no."

It gave instantly.

"What the hell did you do?" I demanded. "Did you ruin it?"

"I just cut the ties. You said you didn't want it."

"I was gonna give it to Val!"

"She can find more lacing. It was gonna take too long to untie."

He pulled the corset off of me, and pulled the light linen blouse underneath over my head.

"What's the hurry—"

He stepped up behind me and slid his hands over my breasts, gently kneading them. They were so warm against the chilled skin.

"This is just going to make everything complicated," I said, even as I instinctively pushed my body closer to him.

"Everything is already fucking complicated," he growled, brushing his thumbs over my nipples, before laying a kiss on each and picking me up. I wrapped my legs around him as he carried me to the bed, that final flimsy petticoat riding up to my hips. "At least this complication can be a fun one."

I couldn't argue with him there. More correctly, I didn't want to argue with him. As he dropped me on my freshly made bed, there wasn't a lot going on in my brain aside from it screaming *yes yes yes* at the sight of him pulling shirt off and revealing his muscled, scarred and tattooed chest, deeply tanned from years of working in the sun.

I didn't think I'd still be this wound up after finally fucking the commodore last night and breaking my long dry spell at last, but I was wrong. Last night had been something new to explore. Sex with Edward Dauntless was comforting and safe. Somewhere I could let my guard down. When we decided to let our egos get out of the way.

A jolt of pleasure raced through me, arcing my back off the bed and bringing me immediately back into my body. Dauntless had run his finger up my damp seam, lingering on the spot of pure pleasure, a location he had memorised.

"You're thinking too hard." His voice was low and deep. "Stay here with me, Magpie. Everything else can wait."

"I was thinking about you," I protested, as he danced his fingers up and down between my folds, teasing my pleasure but sliding away frustratingly soon. He did always like to play. I pulled myself up to sitting, and pulled at his trousers. "Why're you still wearing those?"

"I got distracted by a siren." He slid off the bed, and removed them. Because it wasn't enough that this scoundrel buccaneer was blessed with good locks, he also had a large cock and as soon it was free, it pointed at me like it was a compass and I was north. I took in a breath.

"Save it for some poor maiden who doesn't know all your lines already," I told him, my eyes fixed on his member. He grinned, sly and male. He returned to bed and I climbed onto his lap, his cock trapped between us, hot and twitching with desire. We kissed, hot and messy, his goatee prickling against my face in a familiar way, until he dipped his to my neck and began to pepper me with hard kisses that would surely leave marks. I reached between us, and wrapped my hand around his cock, stroking it fast enough to wring sounds from him that I felt against my neck, but slow enough that it wouldn't end before we were ready. With my mouth, I traced the line of his tattoos with my tongue, and occasionally nipped with my teeth, feeling his cock twitch every time I did so.

I was lost to all thought, so I didn't know how long we'd been like that when he spilled me on my back.

"Enough of this," he growled. "Neptune knows when some scuttling fuckwit will barge in and interrupt before we have our pleasure."

"I'll kill them, I swear it." I don't know how much of my threat was actually intelligible as that was when Dauntless slid one of his fingers into my cavern of delights, and my words were lost to a gasp of surprise and pleasure. My walls tried to clamp down but he was already pulling it out. As he teased me with his finger, his thumb rubbed deft circles on the place he knew would drive me senseless. Delicious jolts of pleasure went straight to my core, adding to the powerful wave building there.

"Now you're the one wasting time," I told him. In response, he only grinned, and slid a second finger alongside the first, my walls stretching slightly to make room, then continuing to thrust them.

"I want to see your pleasure first," Dauntless Dauntless told me, lowering his lips to mine as fingers still worked. "It's been so long since I've seen you lost to complete abandon instead of worrying or arguing."

Arguing with him was suddenly the last thing on my mind at that moment as he thrust a third finger in. My walls spasmed around him stretching in that oddly pleasurable way. His calloused thumb worked the spot of pleasure in an uneven, unpredictable rhythm, driving me towards the edge. The fullness with his fingers was nice but I shivered with anticipation of his familiar cock.

The pent up pleasure inside me was on the brink of tipping over when he flexed his fingers inside me at the same time as sending a bolt of pleasure straight to my centre. Suddenly it was too much, too much to hold inside. My hips rose off the bed and I cried out - it might have been his name, it might have been just noise. The rush of the orgasm shook my body, and in its wake, I felt lighter than air.

I opened my eyes to see Dauntless's dark eyes drinking in the sight of me, still shaking with the after tremors.

"You're fucking beautiful," he told me. He took his out of me, and spread my wetness from his hand onto his cock.

"Fuck me or I'll start arguing." Seconds later, I felt the impossibly hot head of his member at my entrance, then he slid in with no resistance from my body. I gasped, the motion creating starbursts of pleasure across my body, everything still sensitive from my orgasm barely a minute before.

Dauntless looked down at me, not saying anything, but his face held a myriad of emotions: lust, possessiveness, fear and something else too big I didn't want to name. Then lust eclipsed all, as he began to drive into me, our hot, slick flesh becoming one, along with our cries and gasps. Dauntless was a practiced lover, he knew how to angle himself so every thrust brushed just the right spot as he thrust deep into me. Before long my body flew to pieces under the tidal wave of a second orgasm, and I clung to him, my nails cutting into his back, as I whispered, "Edward, Edward, Edward," into his ear.

I felt his release too, thrusts growing erratic, then burying his cock deep inside me with a cry. My body clung to him and I felt the hot rush of his release, his body shaking the whole time, eventually his gasps slowing to long deep breaths. Both of us sated, he collapsed into bed beside me.

37

———

Lying in my bed afterwards, half drowsing in each other's arms as our skin cooled, my mind couldn't help but turn to the future. "This doesn't change anything. Between us, I mean."

I felt him sigh.

"I know, Magpie. You can relax, I know one fuck doesn't make us the power couple of the sea again."

I turned on my side to run my fingers over his chest and see the sharp silhouette of his profile in the low light. "You're taking this awful well."

"I don't know if you've noticed, Magpie, but I'm just fucking glad to have you around at all right now." He squeezed me closer for a second. "Besides," he mused in a devilish tone. "I haven't tried my luck with this Evangeline wench yet."

"Oh, you *bastard.*" I tried to dig an elbow into his side but he dodged, knowing me far too well. His rich laughter was like warm fur on my skin. "She'd eat you alive."

"Not if I ate her first," he teased.

"I ought to throw you overboard," I grumbled, settling back into my nest. "You just fucked me and now you're threatening to seduce my murderous sister."

"It's what you love about me. I'm a rogue." He leaned over and kissed me, a messy, lingering kiss, that made me feel safe, an illusion I desperately wanted to believe.

"Edward, what *am* I going to do tomorrow? I can't leave here without destroying this place, but I don't think we have the firepower. At the same time, anywhere I go, they're just going to come after me. Me, and anyone with me or around me. I'm a danger to everyone I know."

Dauntless shifted in the dark, silent for a few moments. "Even if you *would* agree to leaving the sea and hiding—which I know you won't—it wouldn't matter. They'd keep hunting for you," he mused. "There's only one way to deal with that I can see. Cut the heads off the snakes: Mercer. Haddrick. Grimstead. Only with them gone does this whole thing fall apart."

"Fuck," I spat. "I should've done that while I was there."

"You had more important priorities," Dauntless reminded me, pulling me close. "Even if you got one, hell, maybe two of them, you'd have been killed. And that wouldn't have been worth it."

"It might have been to get rid of two of them."

"Then who, wench, would've told us all this?" Dauntless asked. "And I'm a selfish man. I love a good strategy as much as the next buccaneer, but I love you more."

The words hung in the air for a moment, before Dauntless realised what he'd said.

"Fuck. No. I didn't mean it," he protested. "It's just the cock talking, all right?"

My flint-like heart beat uncomfortably fast. Yeah, I still

loved him. But I didn't want to say the words. I wrapped my arms around his large torso and laid my head on his chest.

"I know what you mean," I said.

There was a long silence.

I listened to his heartbeat. I reminded myself of all the reasons we shouldn't be together. Then unwanted thoughts of lying in bed with the commodore the previous night flashed into my mind.

"I fucked the commodore last night." The words leapt out of my mouth. Now we could have a fight and forget about having *feelings*.

"And he didn't have the decency to rescue you? I'm not half the scoundrel that man is."

"Is that all you're going to say?"

"What do you want, Magpie?" Dauntless stretched. "Am I meant to be outraged? I think your taste is shit, but you're a free woman. You fuck who you want and woe betide any man that thinks he can tell you otherwise."

"You could be a *little* jealous," I muttered.

"Why? You're naked in my arms and he's only got that stick up his ass for company. I think I know which of us is doing better." He buried his lips in my neck, which sent delightful tingles to all the right places.

"We were talking about strategy," I reminded him, trying to change the subject.

"Right." Dauntless did not lift his head from my throat. "The Last Doubloon is where we left everyone. Let's head there, gather up a pirate armada, and return to Port Elizabeth. We'll level the place and take out Mercer, Haddrick and as many Grimsteads as we can."

"Mmm."

"Evangeline isn't your sister, Magpie," Dauntless said,

mistaking my sleepy murmur of assent for doubt. "Just because you shared your mother's belly with her doesn't make her family. *We're* your family. We spill our blood for you, we don't spill your blood. You got that?"

"If you're my family, this is pretty awkward isn't it?" I sat up and gestured at us naked in bed.

He rolled his eyes, and pulled me back down. "Argumentative wench." He wrapped his arms around me. "Now sleep. You need your rest, so you're not such a grump tomorrow."

"I'm a ray of fucking sunshine," I argued, my eyes already shutting. There was a pang in my heart, remembering how often we'd have this exchange when we were together.

I lay with my eyes closed for several minutes, listening to his breathing become even and deep, and feel his body relax. Waiting until he was asleep.

"I love you too, Edward," I whispered. Then I let sleep carry me away.

38

Noon the next day. I stood at the helm of my ship. The wind was favourable. Crew morale was excellent. We'd been sailing towards the Last Doubloon for a good six hours. Sebastian had been warm to me in the morning, despite Dauntless having obviously stayed the night with me—though maybe he just assumed my streak of never getting laid had continued, who knows. Everything was...really, objectively, good.

So I couldn't explain why the uneasiness that had set in when I got dressed in the morning had grown to full blown dread by the time the sun had hit its noon peak. Something terrible was happening, or about to happen. I couldn't explain why I felt that way, and it was irritating the hell out of me.

I probably needed to talk to someone about it. Just in case sorcerous fuckery was afoot. I shouted for Sebastian to come up to the helm.

"Listen, can you grab the wheel for a bit?" I asked, trying not to get distracted by his good looks or the unresolved question marks around him. I had to put a pin in those mysteries until the slightly more deadly ones were resolved. "I have to talk to Val about something urgent."

"Of course." He stepped in to take control of the ship.

I started heading towards the stairs and swayed. My vision began flickering.

"Captain? Are you all right?" I heard Sebastian's voice but it was quickly drowned out by a loud crackling noise.

"Something... in my head..."

"Magpie, can you hear me?" Through the crackling, there was a voice. It was shouting but it was faint. "We need your help. They're going to kill us. They're going to kill me and the commodore."

"Lysander?" I looked down at my wrist. When scooping up a handful of bracelets that morning, I had unwittingly grabbed the magic bracelet Lysander had given me when we were pretending to be the navy—a lifetime ago. I really shouldn't leave magic bracelets lying around my cabin.

"My father. He's going to sacrifice me so he can have my power and my youth. They say the commodore helped you escape, so they're using this as an excuse to take control of the navy. Magpie, if they go through with this, you are in so much danger."

"This is a trap. How do I know it isn't a trap?"

There was only the crackling for a minute.

"You don't," Lysander said, sounding defeated. "If you won't help us, then at least come here and blow this place to smithereens. Sink the ships, turn the fort to Swiss cheese, set everything on fire."

I weighed his words. I thought about him back at Port Elizabeth and how he reacted to things. I thought about what Dauntless said last night, about the heads of the snake.

"We're coming," I promised. "Hold on."

"Be quick," was all Lysander said with words but the dread I'd been carrying all day suddenly lifted.

I blinked to clear my eyes—I'd lost my vision and hadn't noticed—and found that I was slumped on the stairs up to the top deck. Sebastian was calling my name. My adrenaline surged so fast, I thought my heart was going to break out of my ribs, and my legs shook as I raced for the bell to summon all hands before the mast.

"Turn around!" I bellowed. "Turn this ship around, and make sail for Port Elizabeth!"

"Captain, respectfully, what the fuck?" Val emerged from her cabin, her sewing project still clutched in her hand.

"Fuck waiting," I said. "If we sail back to the Last Doubloon, organise, sail back—who knows where they'll all be? Dauntless said to me last night, the best thing to do is cut the heads off of the snake. They were there last night. And I got word they're hanging the commodore to put their own man in charge and that Magnus is sacrificing Lysander to gain even more power. Why give them more time to get more powerful? We strike now. They won't expect it."

"You got word...how?" Val hiked an eyebrow.

"Lysander. Magic."

"Did it occur to you that it might be a trap?"

"Obviously." I threw my hands in the air. "He told me to just burn the whole place down even if we don't save them."

"Cap'n, we're outgunned and the lad knows it. We can't take Port Elizabeth on our lonesome." Smith walked up, puffing ferociously on his pipe.

Shit. He was right. They had navy ships. Haddrick and Mercer ships. The fort.

"Captain, we'd all love to blow that place to Davy Jones'

locker," Ginger, one of Dauntless's former crew said. "And if we had Lysander's sorcery I'd bet on us against any amount of Haddrick and Mercer. But we're just a normal ship now."

The inevitability of Lysander and St Stephen's death settled on me like a freezing mantle. They were going to die and there was nothing I could do to stop it. I wouldn't force my crew into anything they didn't want to do, because my loyalty was to them first. But knowing they were going to die, and that they had called out to me for help, and that I couldn't do anything, made me numb with horror.

"Captain, I believe I can be of assistance," Sebastian called from the helm.

"Are ye a sorcerer too?" Smith yelled, squinting. "Ye seemed like such a normal lad."

"I'm not a sorcerer, no. But I have some skills that may be of use." Well, I guess the pin was coming out of those mysteries a hell of lot sooner than I was expecting.

I sent Whiskey Pete to relieve Sebastian and he joined us on deck.

"So what exactly can you do? And how? I'm getting real sick of people pulling supernatural aces from their assholes." I paused my cranky tirade, and added, "I know you're helping us, I just can't help shake the feeling there's going to be...a *price* for all of this."

Sebastian's face darkened for a moment, a flicker of fear. I wondered what the word meant to him. For me, the word *price* brought back memories of a dream, a dream of fathomless depths and an ancient entity to whom one or both of us already owed a debt.

"I can call on the ocean to move," Sebastian said simply, after a pause. "The ships in the harbour will not be steady enough to fire. We will only need to worry about the fort."

"Are there any catches to this?"

"No. Please trust me."

"No one told me that today is *'please trust me Captain Flint, I promise I'm not bullshitting you'* day." I didn't even pretend I wasn't grumpy. "I'll make sure I put it in my captain's log so we can all celebrate it next year." *If we live that long.* I stepped closer to him and lowered my voice. "Sebastian. You need to explain what all this is. The dreams I've had. I know I got shot and you saved me, somehow. I found the bullet holes in my clothes. You're hiding something."

He bowed his head for a second before meeting my eyes again. "You're right," he said softly, putting one hand over mine. "I haven't been honest with you. I come from an unconventional family—*not* like the Grimsteads," he added, with a gentle squeeze. "Secrecy has been an important part of our lives. But I owe you the truth. Will you wait until after we are done at Port Elizabeth?"

"Wait?" I squawked, sounding more like Dauntless as a parrot than myself. I thought of Lysander and Benedict, and gritted my teeth. I may even have stomped my feet on the deck but I'll shoot anyone who says that. "Fine. But if you die to get out of telling me, I swear by Neptune's balls, I'm going to march into Davy Jones's locker and drag you out by the hair."

Sebastian laughed and shook his head. "Don't make promises you can't keep, Captain Flint."

I turned and looked at the gathered crew. "All right, crew. It turns out we have more aces than a cheater's deck of cards, so we're turning around and showing Port Elizabeth what we're made of. They had something precious of ours and they got off too lightly for stealing her. Now, we're going to sail into the bay and sink every navy ship, every Haddrick and Mercer ship, and blow their fort straight to Davy Jones' locker. Me and whatever mad bastards are willing will go up to the Mercer house and cut the heads off the snakes: Kill Evangeline. Kill Wilfred. Kill Magnus. We won't be safe on the seas until we send them down to old Davy. Aye?"

"Aye aye!" they all shouted.

They're all as mad as I am, and I love them for it.

39

Port Elizabeth was lit up like a pleasure house at low tide when we arrived, with as many ships in the harbour to boot. Three Haddrick and Mercer ships were moored at the loading docks, and three navy ships were anchored in the harbour. The fort on the side of the cliff was lit and manned, bustling like an anthill with red coats.

The shore team consisted of myself, Val, Judith, Dauntless, and Ginger. Dauntless was back in human form since sunset had passed. Val was adamant she would come and take revenge on her kidnappers. Although she was short, curvy and bespectacled, there was a reason her pleasure emporium was one of the safest places in the Caribbean before she'd taken to the seas. She could handle herself. Judith insisted her meagre magic skills would be useful, and Ginger was a long time member of Dauntless's crew who knew how to fight with a sword, gun and fist.

I, of course, was going because this whole hare-brained mission was my ridiculous idea in the first place.

Sebastian insisted that he couldn't do his 'thing' without

us being ready in our longship. Reluctantly I agreed, and we made preparations to go ashore.

He and Smith had command of the ship in my absence. And secretly, Smith had orders to put bullets in Sebastian if he turned on us. I wasn't this paranoid normally, but everyone I'd met with magical powers was a treacherous asshole, bar one—Judith seemed all right.

"Fall right back if you have to," I told them. "Look for our signal that we've succeeded."

"Lass— pardon, captain—how're we to know that?" Smith was smoking a new pipe, having chewed the stem off his last one out of anxiety.

"You'll know. There'll be an explosion, or something equally dramatic."

"And if you don't come back?" Sebastian's eyes did not hold their usual comfort. For a second, they sent a chill down my spine, giving me an echo of those terrible dreams.

"Then leave. Take everyone and head for the Last Doubloon."

"No." Sebastian took me in his arms, gripping me tightly. "I've been waiting and worrying on this ship for you for days."

"If you think I'm going to sit here for you—"

"No, captain. You misunderstand." He smiled, and his smile at least was warm and familiar. "I would never seek to hold you in check. But I won't sit on my hands either. If things go badly, get to the highest point on the island you can. And at dawn, I'll clear the harbour. Even Magnus Grimstead can't fight a tidal wave."

Dauntless, some way behind me, coughed significantly.

"You and I are going to have to have a talk about all this," I told Sebastian. "But I got it. High ground at dawn."

Satisfied, he released me.

I was the last person to lower myself into the longboat. We could just make out Sebastian stepping up to the fore of the ship, as close to the prow as he could. He simply stood with his arms at his sides.

For several minutes nothing happened. Val and I exchanged anxious looks, while Dauntless glowered suspiciously.

How long did we give him before deciding he's actually just delusional? Before I could reach a conclusion, the sea surged underneath us. We grabbed onto the edges of the boat, and each other, as a second surge rippled out.

I glanced up at the fore where Sebastian still stood motionless.

The sea surged directly under the boat and carried us into the harbour. We moved fast, much faster than we could have rowed. It was as though we had a particularly good wind in our sail, only there was no wind, and we had no sail. We ducked as low as we could to reduce our visibility. If we could make it to shore without any cannon fire, it'd be a great start to the night.

"I don't think we're nearly suspicious enough of that Sebastian," Dauntless said, uncomfortably contorting his large frame.

"No, I'm incredibly suspicious. It's just that he's very useful right now," I replied.

"When he worked for me, he told me he was absolutely done with seafaring and refused even to go down to the docks," Val volunteered. "I assumed he was trying to avoid being caught for a crime or being found by his family. You know. The usual reasons people hide out."

I peeked over the edge of the boat. Sebastian, as

promised, was keeping the ships in the harbour too busy to take a shot at us, on account of the maelstrom that had opened near them, forcing them to focus on avoiding the briny whirlpool. The maelstrom that had nearly swallowed Lysander in my cabin popped back into my mind.

"He's certainly made good on his promise that the ships aren't going to shoot us. They're too busy dealing with a maelstrom that Sebastian whipped up," I told them, ducking back into the ship.

"The man can control the sea!" Dauntless hissed. "And he keeps it a secret! Neptune's balls, why is *he* not looking for total dominion of the oceans?"

"Maybe he's not as power hungry as everyone we keep company with?" I suggested. "Val, are you sure you didn't notice anything weird about him? Does he have a full name?"

"It's not going to help, it was something really ordinary," Val said. She thought for a minute. "Jones. Sebastian Jones." She shrugged. "The only thing less helpful would be Smith—"

She was cut off by several enormous bangs.

"Cannonballs!" Ginger called. "From the fort! They've spotted us!"

There were several loud splashes nearby as the cannon balls plummeted into the ocean, missing us completely.

We sat up, hiding no longer useful. I waved in the direction of the fort and then flipped the bird, since somebody was bound to be watching us through a spyglass. I waited for someone to tell me off, then I realised everyone else in the boat was too busy making lewd gestures to do so.

I had exactly one second to bask in the golden glow of being with people who I was so thoroughly in sync with, then there were more enormous bangs. This time, two of the cannonballs hurtled straight towards us.

The words 'abandon ship' were on my tongue, but Judith screeched, threw her hand out in the direction of the cannon balls and shouted a phrase I didn't understand.

A flash of green light and a burst of acrid smoke followed.

Instead of cannonballs, two small, soft things hit us.

I coughed and blinked rapidly, trying to regain my night vision.

There was another boom, but even with my poor night vision I could see we were out of range now, Sebastian's... 'magic,' for lack of a better word, had carried us away faster than the fort could adjust their cannons. We would reach the docks in another minute or two.

"Judith, you did it!" Val exclaimed.

With green lights still dancing in front of my eyes, I looked at what Val was holding up. "Is that a dead parrot?"

"She turned the cannonballs into parrots!" Val clarified. "She's only been practicing the spell for two days!"

"Those books we stole from Magnus had notes for the spell he used on Dauntless. I thought maybe if I learn it, I can eventually figure out how to reverse it. So I've been trying to turn things into parrots. Only, it's quite hard." Judith looked proudly at the second dead parrot in the boat.

Dauntless and Ginger looked horrified.

I tried, and failed, to think of something supportive to say. "But why is it dead?"

Judith looked at me like I was the one asking a ridiculous question. "Cannonballs aren't alive, are they?"

"Aye, they aren't, not yet," I muttered. Maybe that would be a fun surprise later in the evening.

As we pulled up along a dock, the five of us piled out.

A man in fisherman's clothes looked at us. "Ye can't moor here—" His eyes focused on my face. "Yer a wanted woman!"

Three flintlocks and a witch's hand pointed at him. I reached into my pocket and pulled out a coin.

"Everyone wants me and no one can catch me. So listen." I held up the coin. "You shut your mouth, you get this coin and three more when we come back and our boat is still here. If you rat us out, our witch here will put a curse on you. You'll never get your cock up again and you'll die of a painful snakebite before six full moons are through. Isn't that right, Judith."

"I am the mistress of snakes," Judith intoned, rising to the occasion beautifully, "I'll have them stalk you with the waxing and waning of the moons so you know true terror before one finally strikes."

The man held out his hand. "I'm trying to have a son. I can't have my pecker giving up on me. I'll shut my mouth, I promise."

I shoved the coin in his hand and we left him alone, whispering assurances to his member.

We followed Judith through the streets which were getting increasingly crowded.

"What's with the crowd?" I asked, but the citizens of Port Elizabeth weren't much for small talk with strangers.

Val adjusted her breasts, touched a young man on the arm until he looked at her and then repeated my question.

"They're hanging the commodore for treason any minute now. We're all trying to get into the gallows field. We missed out on seeing a famous pirate hang yesterday, not gonna miss seeing a treasonous commodore... Hey, miss, you want some help getting there?"

Val turned away and looked at us.

"Oh, fuck subtlety," I said. Dauntless seemed to agree because the next thing he did was pull one of his flintlocks from his belt and fire it into the air.

"I'm Captain Edward Dauntless, fearsome pirate," he bellowed. "And I do not fucking wait in line."

"Everybody out of the way!" I shouted, brandishing my own guns. "This is a robbery! Your money or your life!"

People scattered, screaming. Nobody noticed we weren't trying to rob anyone.

We sprinted down the road, Dauntless and I at the front, Val and Judith in the middle, Ginger bringing up the rear. Ginger's job mostly consisted of dissuading any good Samaritan who tried to rescue Val or Judith, while Dauntless and I fired the occasional shot and bellowed threats.

We skidded around the corner. There was a man at the gate to Gallows Field. He sized us up and still asked for a ticket.

You have to love the capitalist spirit.

I shot him in the thigh.

Gallows Field was less of a field and more of a crude amphitheatre. Roughly built wooden seats on a natural hillside afforded everyone a clear view of the scaffolding and the prisoner in the noose on the raised platform down the front. The front row was much nicer built than the rest, and even from the back, I could recognise the bulk of Wilfred Haddrick. The towering wig beside him could only be my dear sister. On the scaffolding was some official prick in a wig reading out the crimes, and a hooded executioner standing next to the lever that'd drop the floor out from under the prisoner.

In the noose, looking bedraggled, beaten, bloodied but his dignity unbroken, was Benedict St Stephen.

40

I didn't listen to where the official prick in the wig was up to in reading the charges. I stormed straight down the narrow aisle between the benches, drawing one of my throwing daggers as I ran, and flung it straight at the executioner as soon as I was within range.

It hit the man square in the chest.

I threw a second one that hit him in the thigh. Neither was immediately lethal. That didn't matter. No executioner was paid enough to have the commitment to carry out the job with two daggers sticking out of them.

The man screamed, stumbled and fell backwards off the platform. The guards rushed to check on him, giving zero shits about the prisoner.

Screaming erupted on the field. I heard shots being fired. I leapt up onto the scaffolding, putting my body between the crowd and the commodore—former commodore, I guess— and started loosening the noose.

"Captain Flint." He stared at me the way I'd seen men

stare at things that aren't there when we'd been becalmed and run out of fresh water. "My god. How did you…"

"Short answer, magic." I slipped the noose off him and started hauling him off the platform. "I'll tell you the long answer on the ship tonight."

Thankfully, his hands were tied with rope, so I didn't have to pick a lock in the mayhem. Dauntless and Haddrick were duelling with swords, Dauntless grinning wildly as he insulted Haddrick all the while. I overheard him proclaim "Your father was a baboon." Val clambered over seats, chasing Evangeline. Ginger had taken up position in the seats and was picking off anyone who pointed a gun at us. And Judith was… crouching in a circle in the dirt, chanting?

Well, that didn't bode well.

My attention was quickly diverted by the voice of a man who was wearing the uniform of the commodore—no doubt the newly installed Haddrick and Mercer puppet. He was shouting orders.

Half of the crowd, which had appeared to be made up of entirely civilians, revealed themselves to be navy plants. They drew their weapons, moving towards us at speed.

"I told you the traitor's whore would come," the puppet commodore barked. "He's been in league with her all long."

St Stephen staggered back at those words, as though he had been struck. He turned his face away from his accuser, eyes shut, shame suffusing his features. A shudder ran through him.

"Ignore him," I told Benedict. Guilt burrowed deep into my chest as I saw his humiliation, and how his once-loyal troops turned on him. I'd never meant for this to happen. I never meant to ruin him.

"But he's right." He opened his eyes to look at me. "By my own standards, I deserve this."

The rope fell away from his hands. Just in time, because the navy men were closing in fast.

"The hell you do. They're all morally corrupt liars, don't listen to them." I tried to pull Benedict away but he was frozen to the spot.

"Come on," I yelled, tugging harder. "I can't fight them all!"

Fighting them all was looking like an inevitable possibility.

Well. If they wanted a fight, they were going to get one. By Neptune's beard, they weren't going to kill me running. I put myself between the commodore and the oncoming attackers, drew my guns and grinned savagely.

"Who's gonna be the lucky man, eh?" I crowed. "I'll haunt my murderer for the rest of his life." I lined up two sailors in my sights, ready to go down fighting.

And that's when the horde of feral goats arrived.

41

P andemonium erupted.

It stood to reason that a whole lot of goats would create a whole lot of chaos, but the reality surpassed my wildest imaginings. They were chaotic in ways I could only aspire to. The goats truly cared for no rank or distinction; they gave no shits if you were man, woman, both or neither, if you were an adult or child or in between. The goats followed only their own desire and when there were well over one hundred of these creatures, no force on earth could help you if you stood between them and what they wanted.

And what did these minions of chaos want? Judith, standing in her little circle, looking jubilant.

"I did it!" she shouted. "I called them again!"

"Yes, well done," I called, still protecting the former-commodore as the amphitheatre became a tangled mess of human and animal.

The absolute bastions of stubbornness ran nimbly over the uneven terrain. Being just over three feet tall, their horned heads were perfectly poised to butt people at the waist, folding them in half and knocking them onto the ground, where they were promptly trampled.

The navy men were now too busy trying to fend off goats to worry about us. The new commodore turned murderously towards us. I flipped him off, and then he too was unceremoniously butted to the ground by a particularly large horned specimen.

"Over here!" Val shouted, pointing at the prisoner transport wagon. Either they had repaired the damage from yesterday or they had a second one. It didn't matter to me, a reinforced closed cart was just what the sawbones had ordered.

"Val, Judith, St Stephen, Ginger, inside." I pulled the former-commodore down the stairs with me. He seemed to have found his legs. "Dauntless, up the front with me."

I looked over my shoulder. The people of quality were fleeing, the navy was overwhelmed, and absolutely nobody had time or energy to pay attention to us amidst the mass of rambunctious ruminants fighting to get closer to Judith.

"Captain, do you want me to keep the goats?" Judith bustled towards the cart. "If I keep the spell, they'll just follow us."

"I take back everything bad I said about magic." I passed Benedict St Stephen off onto Judith who pulled him into the cart. "Magic is fantastic and I love it. Absolutely keep the spell."

St Stephen finally pulled his wits together. "What's happening?"

"You're escaping." I gave him an encouraging smile. It was somewhat undermined by loud bleating, swearing and a gunshot from behind me.

"With you," he replied uncomprehendingly.

"It's a strange world, isn't it?" I said blithely. I longed to talk to him properly, but now was definitely not the time. Ginger finally extricated themselves from the mass of goats that was now pressing up against the cart, and climbed in. I smiled at St Stephen again. "You know how I hate to be predictable. Now everyone, hold on tight. It's going to be a bumpy ride."

At the front of the cart, Dauntless was already in the driver's seat holding the reins of the two donkeys hitched to the cart. I jumped up beside him and he flicked the reins urgently, goading the placid creatures into action.

"Thank god one of us knows how to drive on land." I said as I looked up towards the house on the rise, looming over the rest of the island. Extremely localised arcs of violet lightning cracked the sky above it, casting a sinister light. "To the Mercer mansion; We've got a date with a wizard."

WE ARRIVED AT THE MANSION WITHOUT ENCOUNTERING ANY opposition. Either no one could get close enough to take a shot at us over the barricade of billy goats, or they just decided it wasn't worth it. We skidded up to the large front doors, and shot the guards on sight.

I often try to be merciful. Tonight wasn't one of those nights.

Dauntless halted the wagon before the main doors. I threw open the back of the wagon and hopped out to start picking the lock on the manor doors. Judith climbed down and was swarmed by her bleating admirers.

I helped the former-commodore out and made sure he was steady on his feet.

He blinked in surprise at the Mercer house. "What are we doing here?"

"You're not the only person I have to rescue tonight. We have to save Lysander, then we'll take to the seas." I smiled at him, but I knew it was a bitter smile. "You're an outlaw now. Sorry about that. I told you she was the bad sister."

He nodded briskly, his face settling into the solid, dependable lines of implacable justice. He stripped one of the dead guards of his coat and weapons.

"God help me, you're the only person I trust right now." He put on the dead man's coat.

"Touching," Dauntless interrupted. "Has everyone reloaded? We have no idea what we'll find inside."

"Don't be jealous." I double-checked that my flintlock had powder and shot. "We're all on the same side here."

"Unlocked!" Val called. She stood behind us Dauntless kicked the polished wooden doors in with as much strength as he could muster.

We prepared to meet what lay ahead.

42

Nothing.

There was no sound apart from the periodic rumbling of thunder, no startled servants or outraged guards.

"Guess he gave all the servants the night off," I muttered.

"The help does spook when the lord of the manor conducts human sacrifice," Judith noted, as if this was a routine problem in high society. Who knows, maybe it was. I don't know what rich people do.

We didn't waste time ogling the furnishings. Judith and Val knew where Magnus's study was from their previous break-in. As we raced up towards the third floor, traipsing mud, blood and goat dung all over the carpet, it occurred to me we probably didn't need the goat entourage anymore. I said as much to Judith who reluctantly released the spell, leaving the several dozen goats who had followed us in to wander around, nibbling at the wall paper and chewing the carpet.

I allowed myself a moment to picture Angie's outraged face later when she found her house full of goats.

Upstairs, we found the door of Magnus's study unlocked. The overconfidence of wizards is wonderful. It flew open without resistance when Dauntless kicked it in, revealing a large open room. Someone had clearly sacrificed some upstairs bedrooms and interior walls to create it. To one side, there was an area that looked like a study, but that was the area I was least concerned with.

The great big fucking magic circle with three Grimsteads in the middle of it was by far the most dangerous thing in the room.

(Apart from us, of course.)

This magic circle looked like someone had looked at Lysander's shitty chalk circles and asked Val to replicate it but with style and panache. Magic sigils were painted onto the floor in intricate detail and decorated with gemstones, carved rocks, candles, and plants. The whole area was well lit with a dozen massive candlesticks with candles as thick as my arm. It was opulent and completely over the top. I didn't know if it helped with the magic, or if it was just Magnus being dramatic.

Inside the massive circle were three men wearing nothing but dark linen trousers.

My eyes went to Lysander first. He lay on the floor, bound and gagged. Every visible inch of his body was inscribed with strange symbols, in either ink or blood, I couldn't tell. He was struggling, but he was unable to move from where he was placed, owing to a boot on his chest.

Owning the boot, and looking directly at us, was a man that I could only assume was one of Lysander's brothers. He looked older than Lysander but had the same distinctive features: cobalt blue eyes, fine blonde hair, distressingly pale English skin, self-assured smirk.

Beside him stood his father. I wished he were wearing some ridiculous magician robes or something; pasty, old wizard flesh wasn't the most upsetting thing I'd seen tonight but it was up there. He was focused on the book in his hands, lips moving silently to pronounce... something, a spell, a curse. Definitely not a great new recipe for coconut fish. Like Lysander, the older Grimsteads' bodies were covered in symbols.

Great. We were here. Now we just had to figure out what to do.

The air was thick with the smell of incense and that strange smell that accompanies lightning strikes, which were still crackling and booming overhead.

"Are you the rescue team my little brother summoned?" the brother asked. His eyes flicked over us and his lip curled. "Oh, you may have managed to turn the tide at that pirate shanty town last week, but you won't best my father at magic so easily. The circle's warded too well. You can't get in."

"We fucked some Grimstead over with a little re-animated snake, that was pretty funny," I replied. "Eh, Judith?"

Judith was too busy looking at the circle to reply.

From the ugly look that crossed the man's face, I was pretty sure I knew which brother it was. "You won't be able to use that trick again," he bit off.

"Aristides, I presume," I grinned.

I looked to my companions for inspiration, ideas, suggestions. The commodore—excuse me, St Stephen—hung back, staring in horror at the sight before him. I guess it was one thing to know that members of polite society were sorcerers, and another thing to see it for yourself. This was a big step up from Lysander's magic. Judith was fascinated by the circle, and Val was taking everything in in that way she does, not missing a detail. Dauntless was beside me, his face a mask of fury. Ginger was guarding the door, ready to pick off anyone that turned up.

"The circle is warded against physical intrusions as well as the magical intrusions of others," Aristides informed us. "Father is almost done. You will get to witness his rebirth—and his punishment of this abject failure of a child."

There was a flash of purple light, followed by a deafening noise. The house shook. I was nearly thrown off my feet. I grabbed Dauntless to steady myself.

The air now was suffused with a purple light. Magnus's eyes glowed in that same colour. He placed the book down behind him and picked up a long knife, its sharp blade gleaming in the candlelight.

Fuck.

"No!" I shouted, throwing my arms out, only to have them meet solid resistance where the line of the circle was. "Stop!"

I looked at Lysander lying on the floor, his cobalt eyes white around the edges with terror as he looked to me for help. My whole body chilled as the realisation hit me that I was powerless. I couldn't save him.

More importantly, I *wanted* to save him. He was right when he'd told me I was possessive and I considered him mine. Just like Benedict St Stephen was mine, and had been since I pulled him out of his shipwreck.

I screamed in primal rage, and balled my fists so tight that my nails cut into my palms.

I didn't see Dauntless striding forward until it was too late. His jaw was set in a grim determination I knew too well and his gaze was locked on the violet orbs that were Magnus's eyes. His expression was pure hatred.

Alarms went off in my head, he was about to do something dangerous, even if I couldn't guess what.

"Fuck you, Grimstead," Dauntless growled, as he strode purposefully across the sigils and into the circle which, to my enormous surprise, admitted him without protest.

43

There was another deafening crash of thunder as Dauntless entered the circle, and the house rattled from the force of it. Dauntless lived up to his self chosen moniker, and was undeterred even as the rest of us were thrown to the floor.

Magnus was the only other person to remain standing, tightening his grip on the knife in his hand, his eyes glowing and his lips moving soundlessly.

"Of course!" Judith breathed, pushing herself up. "He's cursed by Magnus's magic. Magnus can't ward against his own magic, so the circle won't work against Dauntless!"

Dauntless slugged Aristides hard in the face before he could get to his feet, and then once more for good measure, then turned to Lysander on the ground.

"Break the circle!" I screamed. "Just—kick shit out of the way!"

"I prefer it when I can just shoot problems," Dauntless grunted, picking up Lysander and starting for the edge of the circle.

As if summoned, a shot rang out.

Dauntless balanced for a moment, the life draining out of his face. He crumpled at the knees before falling on top of Lysander, still inside the magic circle. On his back, blood began to pool from the hole in his back.

"It is just easier to shoot people, isn't it?" Aristides said, gun in hand, having pulled it from Neptune knows where.

I screamed, pain and anger and heartache pouring out of me in noise. "*Dauntless!*"

He didn't move.

"Dauntless, you worthless scumbag, *get up*."

My ears roared. Was it thunder again or my blood racing? I've been through the storm of thinking Dauntless was dead once before. I couldn't deal with it again.

Now both Dauntless and Lysander were stuck in a magic circle and there was nothing I could do but watch helplessly from the side. My chest felt like it was cracking in two.

I wasn't expecting Magnus Grimstead to be the person to solve my problem, but he had a flair for the unexpected. It's probably the only thing we have in common.

My pulse pounded in my temples. As I swallowed the rising bile of panic and incense, Magnus Grimstead snapped out of his trance. He took Aristides by the shoulder and cut his throat.

Aristides' death mask of horror clearly showed that he had no idea that was on the agenda.

Magnus shouted several words, his voice echoing around us in an entirely unnatural way, at least until the roar of thunder drowned him out. Purple incandescence enveloped the circle.

I squinted, only just able to make out what was happening within it. The body of Aristides began to shrivel and age, while Magnus's body began to smooth out, grow taller, wider.

He was getting *younger*.

Then Dauntless sat up.

"Fuck, Magpie, what in Neptune's bristly backcrack just happened?"

"Dauntless!" I choked on the words, having inhaled so sharply I got too much incense in my sinuses. "You were *shot*!" I looked at Judith. "I thought he was dead. *Again.*"

"I don't know!" She threw her hands in the air. "Stop asking me difficult questions. I'm new at this. Besides, from Lysander's noises, we should get going."

Lysander was still on the floor below Dauntless, gagged, but making urgently muffled noises.

Dauntless was smarter than me; he asks less questions. He hauled himself to his feet, still visibly confused, kicked the way clear, and dragged himself and Lysander across the sigils and across the barrier of purple light.

The circle was now definitely broken, and the magic felt none too happy about it. Lightning was now inside the house, sparking and arcing wildly off the remains of the circle. Purple zigzags of power lashed out and left burn marks on the floor. Still glowing purple was the air around Magnus and the corpse of his son.

I thought about trying to shoot Magnus but even at this distance, I felt the sheer power rolling off him. I'd be lucky if I didn't die if I took a shot.

"The house is on fire," Val shouted.

I sliced Lysander's bonds and pulled out his gag. "Can you run?"

"From here?" He shuddered. "Yes."

"Then we run," I said.

44

W e didn't bother with the damn cart; we just legged it out the door and straight down the hill as fast as we could. The island was in chaos. The goats had mostly but not entirely dispersed. They were now the least of anyone's problems. The purple lightning was no longer contained directly above the mansion. It was striking all over the island. Several fires had started already. The harbour looked like a mess of broken boats.

I hoped none of the wrecked ships in the harbour were mine.

As the ground under our feet changed from cobblestones to packed dirt, it was beginning to bug me that we hadn't seen any opposition yet.

"Where's all the men yelling *stop her* and *after them*?" I asked, breathing heavily as I ran. As a sailor, I don't get a lot of running in, and right now, fear for my life and the lives of people I cared about was doing a lot of heavy lifting in that department.

"Searching for us would be foolish," the former-commodore said, barely sounding puffed. "They'll have reinforced the fort, secured the upper classes, and be patrolling the docks."

"Oh good. I knew it was too good to think we'd get out of here without a fight."

"Be careful what you wish for," St Stephen said.

"Keep your fucking mouth shut," was Val's version of the same sentiment.

Unfortunately, St Stephen was right. We ran into a group of ten navy sailors, vigilantly looking out for us. So vigilantly, they missed us until the first shot took down one of them. The fight was fast, even with it being two to one in their favour. Judith and Lysander weren't much for fighting, and I think the former-commodore was still struggling with morality, but Dauntless fought as relentlessly as the oncoming tide, taking down five of them on his own.

The look in his eyes frightened me, but now was not the moment to dwell on it. Something had happened to him between the time Aristides's bullet hit him and when Magnus's magic revived him, and he was trying to get it out of his system with violence.

I could certainly relate to that.

Once we had clear sight of the harbour, I sighed with relief. The *Queen's Liberty* was unscathed. The enemy ships were either in ruins or still struggling with the violent waters that had sprung up, to their knowledge, out of nowhere.

Our longboat was within sight. I motioned everyone to hurry, stepping over the dead sailors.

The man I'd paid to watch it was still sitting there. "Told those lads I'd never seen you," he said, his smile gap-toothed and wide as I handed him the promised coins. "Sure is a lot of hullabaloo tonight."

"Only a little of it is my fault," I told him, as everyone loaded themselves onto the longboat.

A shot rang out. The man was blown from his seat into the ocean.

"I hate a liar," the gravelly tones of Wilfred Haddrick pronounced from behind me with the moral certitude of a man who hadn't just committed cold-blooded murder.

I spun around. Haddrick emerged from the shadows between two buildings. I have to presume he'd hid there during the fight like a coward because with his large stature and fine clothes, we couldn't have missed him approaching.

He walked towards me, two pistols aimed squarely at me.

"Why? Because you're too stupid to lie, or you're too stupid to figure out when you're being lied to?" I asked. "Or both?"

His finery looked distinctly worse for wear. I hoped it was from tangling with goats.

"If I'm so stupid, why do I have two loaded guns, while you lot have used up all your shot?" He smiled with undeserved delight. "I saw the fight. You're all empty. I can shoot you, sink the boat, and Angie will stop delaying the wedding."

I grabbed my dagger, preparing to launch at him as he raised his gun.

Before I moved an inch, a massive spurt of blood gushed down Haddrick's leg, immediately drenching his white trousers and pooling at his feet in an alarming volume. I stared at it uncomprehendingly.

Shrieks and cries of astonishment rang out from the occupants of the longboat.

Haddrick's face was pale and growing paler. He tried to say something but managed only a gasp. The guns fell from his limp hands.

Blood poured out of his leg wound, and he slumped to his knees, still looking at me, and I saw the light go out in his eyes.

As he fell face first onto the dock, he revealed an equally pale Georgiana Weatherby standing behind him. She clutched a bloody dagger, her eyes flitting between me and the corpse of Wilfred Haddrick.

"Did I do it right?" she asked, voice cracking.

"Yeah," I replied. My heart was hammering fit to break out of my ribcage. "Couldn't have done it better myself."

"He was going to kill you!"

"You saved my life, kid, I owe you one." This poor slip of a girl had committed murder to save my life. Probably the greatest stain on my soul for quite some time. "Don't lose sleep over him, he was a nasty piece of work. Now get out of here before you get done for the deed."

"I'm coming with you!" Her voice was desperate. "Please. I have to get out of here."

"Do I have to pick up every stray in the caribbean?" I demanded, as I rolled the bulky body of Haddrick off the dock. "Kid, you're the governor's daughter. Can't he keep you safe?"

"I don't know where he is!" Georgiana wailed. "He's been gone for months and Evangeline's kept me here and...I think they've done something to him!"

Oh, Neptune's balls, she was crying now. I shut my eyes. Of course they have. They can't have the governor of the local area getting in their way, can they?

"Get in the boat, kid," I said, as Haddrick's body hit the

water. I mentally consigned him to Davy Jones' locker. "Might as well add kidnapping the governor's daughter to my list of achievements."

"But you're not kidnapping me."

"That's definitely not how they're going to tell it, I promise you." I could already picture the new wanted posters.

I climbed in after her, and we began to row. Lysander was either unconscious or asleep and Dauntless stared grimly ahead as he helped with the oars. Georgiana's teeth chattered from cold or horror or both. Judith put an arm around her.

I looked back at Port Elizabeth—the wrecked ships, the cannonfire that had damaged the fort, the Mercer Mansion burning, and the last remnants of purple light in the sky. I hadn't succeeded in sending this place to Davy Jones' locker as I'd promised. But I'd protected everyone I cared for. My friends were all alive.

And so were all the men I cared about. Even if they were all hurt by what we'd been through.

Sebastian, who came from a family that demanded an unknown price for his power, and threatened to exact it from those he cared for. A family I knew nothing about but who seemed intimately connected to the ocean.

Lysander, who also came from a family of power, whose father saw him as nothing but a tool. He only knew manipulation and deceit but had a deeper, kinder side that I had just begun to glimpse. With his rescue, I hoped I could learn more.

Benedict St Stephen, the former commodore, his world-view broken, his only sanctuary with the very outlaws he chased all his life. Justice deceived him; there was no more black and white view of the world, only endless grey. It could be worse: at least in the dimly lit grey, we could maybe come together.

And Dauntless, the one I know almost as well as myself, who lived up to his name. A reliable scoundrel. Whatever had happened to him in that magic circle scared him bad. And that scared me.

45

B ack on *The Queen's Liberty,* we wasted no time in putting the place to our rudder once again, and sailing away as fast as the winds allowed.

I stood on the top deck with Sebastian, facing the endless ocean before us. The night was clear, so both the sky and the sea were both resplendent in their hues of darkest blue. The sky glittered with an untold number of stars, while the ocean sparkled under the light of a nearly full moon.

I allowed myself to simply exist in the presence of its beauty, after witnessing so much ugliness tonight. I was amazed that the stars and an unspoiled ocean could even share a world with Magnus and Evangeline and their ilk.

After we'd boarded, we'd taken care of everyone as best as we could while beating a hasty retreat. Lysander was in no shape for sorcery. I'd consigned him and the former-commodore to my cabin for rest. I bit my lip. I was really going to have to start calling the former-commodore Benedict.

Dauntless was in my cabin too. He wanted to be away

from people. I guess I was hosting a big sleepover again. Truth be told, I was much happier about the prospect now than I had been the first time.

Val came to my side where I stood admiring the view.

"I've made Georgiana comfortable in my cabin," she told me.

"Thanks," I said. "Any idea what to do next? I'm fresh out."

"Yes, actually." She adjusted her glasses. "You're not going to like it though."

"Can't be worse than the last few days."

"I think we need to go back to the nuns."

"Nooo," I whined, very un-piratelike. In my defense I was very tired and those nuns were very mean.

"They have to know something about your family, or at the very least who put you there." She turned to me, her eyes sharp. "Because either someone lied to Evangeline about you being dead, or she lied to you. You aren't dead, and someone had to have put you in that convent. That someone can provide information."

The witty retort I was definitely about to make was cut off by the ship pitching beneath us, before it came to a complete stop in the water.

"What the fuck?" I turned to Sebastian. "I swear to Neptune, if that's Lysander messing about…"

"It's not," Sebastian's expression was normally comforting but right now, his eyes blazed with fear. "I'm sorry. I believe this is my fault."

"Sebastian…" I turned to see what his horrified gaze was directed at.

A wall of water had risen directly in front of us, a glossy

satin curtain shimmering in the moonlight. It would have been beautiful if it hadn't been utterly terrifying.

A face appeared in the wall, as tall as the mast, resembling an old man with craggy features and a large beard.

"Sebastian," the voice moaned like wooden hulls fighting against a storm. "Captain Flint."

Over the top of my heart pounding, I was vaguely aware that my crew were screaming. I didn't blame them. I wanted to be screaming, too.

"What's it to you?" I heard myself yelling back, because my mouth operates even when disconnected from my brain.

"Magpie, don't," Sebastian murmured.

"My son has abused his powers on your behalf one too many times," the voice like the roar of the tides said. "Time has come for recompense."

"Your *son?*" I looked at Sebastian. I definitely shouldn't have put a pin in the questions around Sebastian, I should have dealt with them sooner. He just seemed so nice, I never would've guessed his dad was even more frightening than Magnus fucking Grimstead.

Sebastian refused to meet my eyes. "I'm sorry," he whispered, his hand finding mine and clutching it tightly. "I'm sorry."

"It is time for us to meet, Captain Flint," the voice continued, like sails whipping in a storm. "Earlier than expected."

The ocean below the ship parted, revealing a whirling funnel of water leading into a watery abyss. The ship lurched again and began sailing into it, heading into the darkness of the deeps.

"No! Your quarrel is with me and Sebastian, no harm must come to my crew!"

Everyone on deck was screaming in terror, and holding

on for dear life. I grabbed Val's arm, and felt Sebastian wrap his arms around me.

"I'm not the one that takes things that do not belong to me," the voice of crashing storms said. With that, the sky was blotted out as water crashed over the ship.

"No!" I shouted. Val was torn from my grasp by the swirling waters.

Sebastian held me tightly, enveloping me with his body. "We'll be safe. You, me, the crew. I swear it."

I couldn't reply as salt water rushed over me. I clung to Sebastian, feeling the ship bear down towards the ocean floor, heading straight towards...

Fuck.

I knew exactly who we were dealing with and who Sebastian's father was.

We were headed straight to Davy Jones' locker.

THANKS FOR READING!

Thank you for reading *Pirate Queen's Revenge!* I hope you enjoyed the book. If you have a a few minutes, I would love it if you would leave an honest review on either Amazon or Goodreads.

To hear about further adventures of Magpie Flint on the high seas, as well as extra content like bonus scenes, sign up to my mailing list, or follow me on Facebook. Scan the QR code for links!

See you aboard *The Queen's Liberty* soon, in *Pirate Queen's Quest!*

ABOUT THE AUTHOR

Isolde Holyoake saw Muppet Treasure Island at an impressionable age, and Tim Curry's excellent Long John Silver convinced her that fictional pirates are the coolest. She knows Pirates of the Caribbean almost word-for-word, celebrates Talk Like a Pirate Day every year and has recently accomplished her dream of having a really impressive hat.

In addition to pirates, Isolde likes vampires and regency gentlemen. She's partial to wearing dramatic coats and enormous dresses (usually not at the same time). She's an avid reader, and enjoys playing video games and running role-playing games. She lives on a sub-tropical island at the bottom of the world, where coffee and cats give her life.

She has no idea how to sail, or swim, so all her nautical adventures have to be imaginary.